WHAT AT FIRST ~~SEEMED TO BE NO~~
MORE THAN SEAWEED MOVED
SENSUOUSLY ON THE WATER'S SURFACE

It was a distinctive three-carat diamond that finally caught the light, broke it into a hundred shimmering rays, and removed any lingering doubts about the exact nature of Molly's discovery.

"Oh, my God," Molly whispered, her gaze fixed on the glittering ring that she herself had once coveted at a charity auction.

Michael's arm circled her waist. The flashlight wavered in his grasp and the light pooled at her feet. "Are you okay?" he asked.

"As well as anyone would be after discovering another body. I suspect I've seen almost as many murder victims as you have in the past few months."

"Don't you think you're jumping to conclusions?"

"Trust me," Molly said. "Tessa Lafferty would never willingly ruin her hairdo, to say nothing of her designer gown. If she felt ill, she would go home, send the dress to the secondhand store on consignment, and then climb between her two-hundred-dollar sheets and die. If she's in that water, it's because someone heaved her into the bay."

Other Dell Books by Sherryl Woods

HOT PROPERTY
HOT SECRET

A MOLLY DEWITT ROMANTIC MYSTERY

HOT MONEY

SHERRYL WOODS

A DELL BOOK

Published by
Dell Publishing
a division of
Bantam Doubleday Dell Publishing Group, Inc.
1540 Broadway
New York, New York 10036

ISBN: 0-440-21485-8

Printed in the United States of America

Published simultaneously in Canada

August 1993

10 9 8 7 6 5 4 3 2 1

RAD

Nature is pleased with simplicity, and affects not the pomp of superfluous causes.

Isaac Newton

CHAPTER

ONE

As Molly DeWitt listened to two elegantly clad women scheme to take a Miami philanthropist to the monetary cleaners, she tried to recall exactly how her neighbor and best friend, Liza Hastings, had managed to talk her into showing up for this black tie charity affair. The last thing she remembered clearly was saying an emphatic no.

That had been a month ago. The next day the fancy, embossed invitation had appeared in her mailbox. A week after that, Liza had begun dropping pointed hints about her failure to reply, especially when the cause was so worthwhile—saving the spotted owls in Oregon and Washington, among other endangered creatures.

"I replied. I said no," Molly recalled saying quite clearly.

1

The ensuing discussion about the responsibilities of friendship had lasted no more than one or two weighty moments. Then Liza had left her to wage a battle with her conscience.

It wasn't that Molly had no conscience. It was simply that she'd grown up attending lavish affairs like this and had sworn on the day of her debut that she never would again. It had always seemed to her that if the women in the room had donated an amount equivalent to the cost of their gowns, there would have been no need for a fund-raiser at all. She could recall mentioning that to Liza on a number of occasions. Liza, unfortunately, had very selective hearing and a skill at arm-twisting unrivaled on the professional wrestling circuit.

The clincher, of course, had been Liza's persuasive appeal to Michael O'Hara. For a hardnosed, macho homicide detective, the man had the resistance of mush when it came to saying no to a woman as committed to a cause as Liza was. He'd looked shell-shocked as he'd written out his sizable check.

"What are we doing here?" he asked now as he nabbed another glass of champagne from a passing waiter.

Molly thought he sounded rather plaintive. She scowled at him. "We wouldn't be here if you hadn't succumbed to Liza's pressure. You had

2

your checkbook out and those tickets in your hands before she even finished saying *please*."

"You could have stopped me."

"How was I to know you intended to drag me along with you? For all I knew you planned to ask that charming go-go dancer who was all over you at Tío Pedro's a few weeks ago."

He grinned. No, actually he smirked.

"Go-go dancer? Your claws are showing, Molly. Marielena is in the chorus of a Tony Award–winning musical on Broadway."

"Whatever."

"Besides, I was hardly likely to ask her when this is your friend's event. I'm almost certain Liza indicated this was a package deal—you and the tickets, all for a paltry five-hundred-dollar contribution." He groaned. "Do you know how many tickets to Miami Heat games I could buy with that?"

"Don't tell me. Tell Liza. I'm wearing a dress that cost nearly double that."

"I thought a former debutante would have an entire collection of ball gowns."

"I do. In size four. I'm an eight now," she said, giving him a warning glare, "and if you make one single snide remark about how I could have starved myself back into those fours, I will personally dump the next tray of champagne I see over your head."

3

He regarded her curiously. "Are you always this charming at galas?"

Molly felt a momentary pang of guilt. She squashed it. "I get testy when I spend more than a week's pay on a dress that with any luck I will not wear again in this lifetime."

"At least you can save it for the Academy Awards or the Emmys, even the Miami Film Festival. Surely in your position with the film office sooner or later you'll have to drag it out again. Where is a cop supposed to wear a tux?"

"Save it for your wedding," she shot back. Considering Michael's avowed status as an eligible bachelor, it was as close to a curse as Molly could come. The alarm in his eyes improved her mood considerably. She linked her arm through his. "Toss down the last of that champagne and let's go mingle."

Actually, now that she was beginning to resign herself to an endless, tedious evening of polite chitchat and lavish praise of the canapés, Molly discovered that she could appreciate the setting, if not the reason for her presence.

For the event Liza had commandeered Vizcaya, the closest thing Miami had to a palace. Built on a grand Italian Renaissance scale between 1914 and 1916, the former winter home of industrialist James Deering faced Biscayne Bay, which dutifully shimmered like a sea of diamonds under the full moon. A soft breeze, laced with the tang of salt air, swept over the estate. Most of the crowd was milling around under a striped refreshment tent on the south lawn or walking through the surrounding gardens, as formal and lavish as any in Europe, no matter that the gatehouse across the road now served as Molly's own office.

The romantic setting was perfect for stealing kisses or seducing the high rollers into parting with their money. Molly caught sight of Liza amid a cluster of Miami's well-to-do socialites, including the event's chairwoman, Tessa Lafferty. They were all preening for the photographer from the morning paper. Liza's dramatic, off-beat dress in a shade referred to as tangerine—at least in the produce section, if not on the fashion pages— looked as out of place in the midst of all those pastel beaded gowns and stiff hairdos as a bold bird of paradise would among sweet and fragile magnolia blossoms.

As she and Michael got close enough to identify the women with Tessa, Molly guessed they would ante up a good thousand dollars apiece before Liza let them escape. Most would consider it a small price to pay to have their friends see them on the society page a few days from now.

Molly watched in amusement as Liza went into her hard sell.

"How does she do that?" Michael asked in wonder as checks and promises changed hands.

"Liza has no shame when it comes to protecting the environment and any critter living in it. She will grovel if she has to."

"How much do you figure an event like this will net?"

"Fifty to seventy-five thousand, maybe more," she said as Michael's eyes widened. "If Liza had actually chaired the event, she would have tried to lure a couple of celebrities into town. With a little star power and maybe one of those fancy silent auctions, she could have doubled the profits. A shindig like this in Los Angeles could pull in a cool million."

"The soccer team raised seventy-five dollars at a bake sale last month and considered it a coup," he said. "Why didn't Liza go for the big bucks?"

"Because, as I understand it, the chairwoman did not take kindly to suggestions from her committee."

"The chairwoman is an egotistical idiot," Liza muttered under her breath as she joined them just in time to catch the gist of their conversation.

"She did manage to get all the uppercrust scions of the oldest Miami families to turn out," Molly reminded her, pointing to the women who still surrounded the chairwoman.

"Sure, but she ignored the rest of the community," Liza countered. "If a few of us hadn't set out to corral people like you and Michael, we would have had to have a nurse on duty to hand out vitamins at the door or the whole crowd would have fallen asleep by nine."

"Don't you think you might be exaggerating just a little bit?" Molly asked. "You're just miffed because you wanted Julio Iglesias to sing and she'd never heard of him."

"Forget Julio Iglesias. I doubt I could have talked her into inviting Wayne Newton. When I mentioned holding an auction, she practically choked. She claimed it had no class." Liza stood on tiptoe to kiss Michael's cheek. "Thanks for coming, you two. Mingle. Have fun. I've got to go see if I can get old man Jeffries to cough up a few thousand bucks before he dies. I've heard he's willing to save the manatees. Maybe I can get him together with Jimmy Buffet and put together a benefit concert."

Liza disappeared around a hedge, leaving the two of them staring after her.

"Where does she find the energy?" Michael marveled.

"I think it takes about twenty minutes and the mention of a cause to recharge her batteries." Molly glanced up. "Are you interested in checking out the food?"

He shook his head. A wicked gleam lit his dark brown eyes. "Not right now. I'm more in the mood to shock this stuffy crowd."

"Oh?" Molly replied cautiously. The last time Michael had that look in his eyes he'd kissed her senseless. It had played havoc with her already wavering resolve to keep this man at arm's length.

"Follow me."

He held out his hand, and after a momentary hesitation, Molly took it. "Exactly what do you have in mind?"

"I intend to start by removing selective pieces of clothing."

She stopped in her tracks. "You what?" It wouldn't do to get too elated under the circumstances. She had a discouraging feeling he wasn't about to lure her into one of the mansion's many bedrooms and have his way with her, thereby settling the matter of her resolve once and for all.

He grinned. Those wicked sparks intensified. "Scared, Molly?"

"Of you? Never!" she declared staunchly.

"Then let's go."

As they crossed the lawn, stopping several times along the way to chat, Molly's pulse reached an anticipatory rate that would have her in the hospital down the block if it continued unchecked. The music drifted on the night breeze, swirling around them. The slow, romantic beat was counterpointed by laughter that grew more distant as they reached the shadowy fringes of the estate. Michael's hand curved reassuringly around hers.

"Put your hand on my shoulder," he instructed, standing before her. "Lift your foot."

"Is this anything like that game where you put different body parts on different squares until everyone ends up on the ground in a tangle?"

"Sounds fascinating," he said, "but no." He removed her shoe and tucked it in his pocket. "Other foot."

"Michael, I do not intend to romp around this place barefooted."

"Careful, amiga. Your stuffy social graces are showing."

In return for that remark, she nearly planted her remaining spiked heel atop his foot. Unfortunately, as a volunteer soccer coach, to say nothing of being witness to a fair amount of gunplay, Michael possessed reflexes that tended to be lightning quick. He stepped nimbly aside. Molly's heel dug into the dry, sandy soil, which effectively removed her shoe just as he'd intended in the first place.

He glanced at her stocking-clad feet. "How about those?" he inquired of the sheer, iridescent hose that shimmered against her legs.

"Is this one of those kinky things I've read about?"

"Last I heard there wasn't anything kinky about sitting on a dock by the bay, but I'm game if you want to show me."

"You would be," she muttered darkly, trying not to let her disappointment show. Kinky with Michael O'Hara might have had its good points.

She wasn't about to be the one to initiate it, though. She glanced at the limestone ledge, worn smooth by time, then at the water lapping gently against it. "You don't actually expect me to sit on that, do you?"

"Of course not," he said, sweeping off his jacket and spreading it before her.

Molly had a hunch the gesture wasn't entirely due to gallantry. In fact, she was almost certain she heard him sigh with relief as he shed the hated, restrictive attire. She glanced from Michael to his quite probably ruined jacket, then to the water that seemed ominously dark in this shadowed corner.

"What do you suppose is in there?"

"A little seaweed. A few fish. Nothing to worry about."

"Maybe you don't consider having barracuda nibbling at your toes to be risky, but I'm not all that enchanted with the idea."

"I doubt there are any barracuda lurking down there."

"Not good enough," she said. "I want conviction in your voice or my toes stay on land."

"Ah, Molly. Where's the romance in your soul?" he murmured, just close enough to her ear to give her goosebumps. His finger trailed along her neck, then over her bare shoulder.

Molly shivered and halfheartedly wished she'd selected a gown with more fabric. She was entirely too responsive and Michael was entirely too skilled at this seduction stuff. Another five minutes and the society grandes dames truly would have something to shock the daylights out of them. As an alternative, Molly practically dived for the ledge. She stuck her feet, outrageously expensive stockings and all, into the bathwater-warm bay.

Michael's amused chuckle was entirely too predictable. As he sat down next to her, she considered—for no more than an instant—tumbling him into the bay so he could cool off his . . . libido.

As if he guessed her thoughts, he grinned at her. "Don't even think about it," he said.

"What?" she inquired innocently.

Suddenly something brushed past her foot, ending all thoughts of retaliation. As it made contact again, it became clear that it was something considerably larger than a guppy or even a damned barracuda, she thought as a scream rose up in her throat and snagged.

"What—" she asked in a choked voice. "What is that?"

"What is what?" Michael said, instantly alert to the change in her voice.

She was already standing, water pooling at her feet as she pointed at the murky depths. "There's something in there."

"Probably just some seaweed."

"I don't think so. It felt . . ." She was at a loss for an accurate description. "Slimy."

"That's how seaweed feels," he said, sounding so damned calm and rational she wanted to slug him.

"Does it also feel big?" she snapped.

"Big like a manatee?" he said, obviously refusing to share her alarm. "Maybe one is tangled in the mangroves."

Molly wasn't sure exactly how she knew that Michael was wrong, but she was certain of it. "Maybe we should go get a flashlight."

"By the time we do, I'm sure whatever it is will be gone."

"Michael, humor me. If it is a trapped manatee, we ought to free it or Liza will never forgive us. If it's . . ." She swallowed hard. "If it's something else, we ought to do, hell, I don't know. Just get the flashlight. I'll wait here," she said before she realized that she'd be left alone with something that every instinct told her was very human and very dead.

Michael had taken two steps back toward the house, when she grabbed his arm. "Never mind. I'll go for the flashlight. Give me the car keys. You stay here."

His expression suddenly serious, he handed over the keys without argument, either to humor her or because his own highly developed instincts for trouble had finally kicked in. "Don't say a word to anyone, Molly. There's no point in alarming everyone unnecessarily."

She nodded, then took off across the lawn, oblivious of the stares she drew as she raced barefooted through the guests, across the central courtyard of the house and down the driveway to the parking lot. It could have taken no more than ten minutes, fifteen at the outside, but it felt like an eternity before she made it back to where Michael was waiting. She'd grabbed a glass of champagne and chugged it down on the way. She had a hunch she was going to need it.

Michael took the flashlight from her trembling grasp and shone it onto the water in front of where they'd been sitting. At first it seemed she must have been mistaken as the glare picked up no more than a few strands of seaweed, a tangle of mangrove roots, a curved arm of driftwood. As the light skimmed across the surface and back again, Molly's heart suddenly began to thud.

"There," she whispered. "Move it back a little. See?"

What at first seemed to be no more than seaweed moved sensuously on the water's surface. It was a distinctive three-carat diamond that finally caught the light, broke it into a hundred shimmering rays and removed any lingering doubts about the exact nature of Molly's discovery.

"Oh, my God," Molly whispered, her gaze fixed on the glittering ring that she herself had once coveted at a charity auction. Though her stomach was pitching acid, she forced herself to look again, just to be sure.

Michael's arm circled her waist. The flashlight wavered in his grasp and the light pooled at her feet, instead of on the water. "Are you okay?" he asked.

"As well as anyone would be after discovering another body," she said in an aggrieved tone. "For someone not even remotely interested in signing on for homicide investigations, I have a nasty suspicion I've seen almost as many murder victims as you have in the past few months."

"Don't you think you're jumping to conclusions? We have no way of knowing whether the woman was murdered until we get the body out of there."

"Trust me," Molly said. "Tessa Lafferty would never willingly ruin her hairdo, to say nothing of her designer gown. If she felt ill, she would go home, send the dress to the secondhand store on consignment, and then climb between her two-hundred-dollar sheets and die. If she's in that water, it's because someone heaved her into the bay."

"I know that name. Wasn't it on the invitation to this shindig?" Recognition spread across his face, then dismay. "Isn't Tessa Lafferty the woman Liza described as an idiot?"

She glared at him. "What are you suggesting?"

"Nothing. I'm just asking, purely for purposes of clarification, if it's the same woman."

"It is," Molly conceded, then jumped to her
friend's defense. "But Liza would never kill her
just because she didn't want some Latin singer
that Liza has the hots for to sing at this bash."

"Did I say she would?"

"No, but I know how you think."

"Do you really? How is that?"

"Like a cop."

"Then I suppose you won't mind obeying an
official police request."

She regarded him warily. "Which is?"

"Go into the house and call the police."

"You are the police."

"Not here. Will you just go make that call?"

"Only if you promise that Liza will not be on
the list of suspects you turn over to the Miami
police."

"Sweetheart, you and I are on that list of suspects. Now move it."

Molly didn't waste time arguing that they provided tidy alibis for each other. She was more concerned with warning Liza that inviting a homicide
detective to a charity function was just about the
same as inviting trouble.

CHAPTER
TWO

With Michael's hand clamped firmly around her wrist, Molly was more or less obligated to leave the murder investigation in the hands of the proper authorities, members of the Miami Police Department who arrived with sirens blaring. Damn the man, beyond insisting that everyone remain on the grounds and seeing to it that the security guards enforced the rule by barricading the routes to the parking lot, he didn't ask a single question of anyone himself.

"It's not my jurisdiction," he said for the tenth time when Molly mentioned that a few casual inquiries surely wouldn't offend the Miami police.

What she didn't say was that asking a few questions would help to keep her mind off the image of Tessa's body being untangled from the mangroves, then placed rather indelicately on the bank awaiting further examination by the medical examiner before its removal from the grounds. Tessa hadn't been in the water long enough for her body to be distorted or ravaged by fish as it might have been had she remained undiscovered, but that didn't make it any less distressing to see her poor, bedraggled, lifeless form lying there. Because she needed a distraction, Molly pressed Michael for some sort of action.

"But what about Liza? Don't you feel any obligation at all where she's concerned? I don't even know where she is. Shouldn't we at least find her?"

"Any obligation I feel toward your friend was pretty well wiped out when I forked over the money for the tickets to tonight's affair."

Molly scowled at him. "That was not the sort of obligation I was talking about."

"I know," he said succinctly.

Refusing to admit aloud that she was worried by Liza's inexplicable absence ever since the discovery of the body, Molly pleaded, "At least let me find her and talk to her. She's bound to be distraught. Who'll want to donate more money to all these environmental causes after this?"

"From what I hear, any publicity is good publicity when it comes to raising public awareness of a cause."

"Spoken like someone who's taken PR one-oh-one. I know there are those who believe that as long as the name is spelled correctly, public relations benefits will be reaped, but I'm not sure that applies to a murder investigation. If this gets ugly, the coalition that sponsored tonight's event is bound to be tainted by it. Besides, Liza is my friend. I want to be supportive."

She also wanted very much to be reassured that Liza had spent the last hour or so in the midst of this throng and not off on one of her solitary nature hikes around the grounds. She left that thought unspoken. Michael was sharp enough to figure it out anyway, just as he'd noticed the handful of yachts docked at the boat landing and notified the guards to block that route of escape as well. Now, unless someone dived into Biscayne Bay and swam away, the suspects were pretty well contained on the grounds. She didn't want to think about how far away the killer might have gotten in that time before the body was discovered.

"Molly, just let the police solve this case as quickly as possible without any of your amateur interference. That's the best thing you can do for Liza," he said.

"I thought you said my instincts about these things were good."

"Did I say that?"

"Just a few short weeks ago, as a matter of fact."

"I must have been in a state of shock after seeing you heading straight into the clutches of that film director's killer. Close calls always muddle my thinking."

"Michael!"

"Molly!"

"Oh, never mind," she grumbled. "I'll wait right over there."

He grinned. "No. You'll wait right here, with me."

If she'd been five years old, she would have sulked. As it was, she stuck with what she hoped would appear to be nothing more than mild disappointment.

"I'll make it worth your while," Michael added.

She regarded him doubtfully. "How?"

He touched one finger to her chin, tilted it up, and covered her mouth with his. The kiss—or maybe it was simply shock—took her breath away. Michael was not prone to public displays of affection, unless she counted the one time she'd seen him patting his ex-lover's fanny in parting. As a result, she wasn't wild about the intent behind the kiss. She had a feeling it had less to do with seduction than it did with distraction. Whatever the dubious intention, however, it momentarily wiped the murder out of her mind. Right at the moment, she couldn't ask for more than that.

"Isn't this a conflict of interest or something?" she murmured eventually, her back pressed against wallpaper that the guidebook she'd picked up indicated was some nineteenth-century French woodblock pattern.

"Not that I know of," he said. "For once we're both on the same side and operating in the same official, or should I say unofficial, capacity."

"But you are a policeman, despite the fact that you aren't on duty, and you did discover the body."

"You discovered the body," he corrected. "I just happened to be around at the time."

"A technicality. Michael, aren't you the least bit curious about what's happened here tonight?"

"Curious, yes. Anxious to get involved, no. You seem to forget I have a caseload as tall as the Freedom Tower as it is. I don't need to chase ambulances, like some starving attorney. You also seem to forget that every time *you* stick *your* nose into one of these incidents, your ex-husband and your boss go through the roof. Do you enjoy taunting them?"

"Hal DeWitt and Vincent Gates have absolutely nothing to do with this. Liza is my friend and I want to help her solve this thing quickly so she can minimize the damage to the cause. It's rare to get a coalition of environmentalists all working together this way and I want it to be successful for Liza's sake. Maybe I even owe it to Tessa Lafferty, too," she said, warming to the noble sound of that.

"Why? Because you didn't contradict Liza when she described the woman as an idiot, a statement, I might add, that could put your friend on the short list of suspects? I read all the time about the nasty, vicious competitiveness that fund-raising spawns. Vizcaya itself got its share of headlines just a year or so ago because two groups of supporters couldn't agree on anything. You're not on this committee. You're not responsible for your friend's actions. Therefore, as far as I can see, Tessa Lafferty's death has nothing to do with you. Play it smart for once and keep it that way."

Molly realized she couldn't very well tell him she was feeling guilty because she herself had coveted that diamond ring Tessa was wearing. She vaguely recalled from long ago Sunday school lessons that coveting what your neighbor had was a significant sin. It was probably not one that a man who dealt in homicides could relate to very easily. Admittedly, it was also a pretty flimsy excuse for involvement in a murder investigation. Protecting Liza was another matter altogether. Liza had stood by her when she'd been under suspicion in the murder of their condo president. Molly owed it to Liza to do the same for her now.

Momentarily thwarted from doing any significant, obvious sleuthing, however, she gazed around the central courtyard where the police had gathered everyone who fit into the open space. Others were crammed into the surrounding rooms, much to the distress of the museum's curator. A few guests had been allowed onto the terrace under the watchful eye of two policemen.

With Michael looking on, Molly moved through the crowd, conducting what she hoped was a casual search for Liza. When she finally spotted her across the terrace going over the guest list with a uniformed officer, Molly sighed. "Thank God," she murmured.

"You didn't really think she'd skipped, did you?" Michael asked, clearly surprised by her apparent lack of faith.

"No, of course not," she said loyally.

He regarded her intently. "Molly, was something going on between Liza and the Lafferty woman that the police should know about?"

"Absolutely not."

"Molly?"

"You already know Liza detested her. Isn't that enough?"

"I suppose," he said skeptically.

Desperate to change the subject, Molly pointed out Tessa's husband to Michael. "See. He's right over there. Isn't the husband always the prime suspect in a case like this?"

Sixty-year-old Roger Lafferty didn't look like a

man who'd just committed a murder. He looked stunned. He was sitting on a stone bench, surrounded by friends. His normally jovial, round face looked suddenly tired and crumpled, as if all of the air had been squeezed out of him.

"How was the marriage?" Michael asked.

"Okay as far as I know, though how he managed to stay married to her is beyond me. From what I've heard, Tessa was not easy to live with even before she turned menopausal. Since then, she's been a holy terror."

"What about the other guests? Was she feuding with any of them?"

Molly was thrilled with the question, not because of the content but because it was proof that he was getting hooked after all. It was possible to take the cop out of his uniform, but obviously he couldn't shut off his analytical mind.

"Jason Jeffries," she said at once, seizing the first name that popped into her mind. She wondered why. She barely knew the philanthropist, though she certainly knew his reputation for largess. Lines from needy organizations practically formed outside his office, like starving ants parading toward a bowl of sugar.

"The man Liza expects to hand over big bucks to save the manatees?" Michael said.

"That's the one."

"He's here tonight?"

"Right over there," she said.

23

Jason Jeffries had pinned the detective in charge of the investigation against a pillar. That was no mean feat, given Detective Larry Abrams's impressive stature and the fierce gleam in his eyes. Jeffries had him cornered all the same and was demanding that everyone there be released immediately.

"Not bloody damn likely," one policeman just behind Molly muttered wearily when he overheard the demand. "We'll be lucky if we get out of here by dawn."

Thank God she'd had the foresight to arrange for Brian to stay overnight with a friend, Molly thought. There would be no need for her son to know about the murder before morning when she could tell him herself. Relieved on that point, and before Michael could stop her, she turned to the officer.

"So," she began as casually as if she were merely inquiring about the weather. "What's the cause of death? Has the medical examiner determined that yet?"

"You'll have to wait for that information, just like everyone else," he said stiffly.

Molly interpreted that to mean he didn't know.

"I heard she was strangled," a woman standing just behind Molly said in a conspiratorial whisper. Though she was a tiny, birdlike woman, she cast a defiant look at her scowling husband, a

24

man Molly recognized as the chief financial of-ficer for one of the remaining solvent banks in town.

"Shut up, Jane," Harley Newcombe snapped. "I doubt whatever you overheard in the ladies' room came from the medical examiner.

"Women are nothing but a damn bunch of gossips," he added, looking to Michael for sympa-thetic support. He glared at the hapless Jane again. "I told you we had no business coming tonight. These people all hate each other. There was bound to be trouble of one sort or another."

Michael's gaze narrowed. "What do you mean, they all hate each other?"

"The infighting in this crowd, especially among the wives, makes one of those high-profile family feuds over money look like sandbox bicker-ing. I never saw anything like it before in my life. You think men play down and dirty in business? That's nothing compared to the way these women go at it."

He shook his head in obvious male bemuse-ment at women's ways. Molly was tempted to point out that at least half of the people at this affair and on the board of the charitable organi-zations involved were men, but Michael had latched on to a skimpy clue and clearly intended to shake it until it yielded real evidence. She was so grateful for that she kept her mouth clamped firmly shut.

"Was Tessa Lafferty involved in the feuding?" he asked.

"Hell, she's the one who started it from what I've heard," Newcombe said, his disgust evident. "Typical catfighting when you get a bunch of women together."

"Harley Newcombe, that is not so," his wife retorted with unexpected spunk, saving Molly the trouble. "It's the men who stuck their noses into things and made everything complicated. That horrible, overbearing Jason Jeffries has to control everything he's involved with. He treated Tessa like she didn't have a brain in her head."

"Why shouldn't he treat her any way he damned well pleases? He's coughing up most of the money."

"He gave a single donation—" she began.

"For a hundred thousand."

"And that entitles him to run things? This coalition had raised three times that before he ever got involved. If you ask me, that awful man is trying to buy his way to sainthood. It's probably penance for some horrible sin he's committed in the name of the almighty dollar."

"Just drop it, Jane. You don't know what the hell you're talking about. If you could manage money, I wouldn't be covering all those bounced checks of yours every month."

Since it was clear that the conversation was rapidly disintegrating into a familiar family squabble, Molly again turned her attention to the generous, if difficult, Jason Jeffries. She spotted him lurking in the shadows near the buffet table, apparently consoling himself with food after his failure to get his way with the detective.

Obviously a man who'd ignored physicians' warnings about obesity, cholesterol, and smoking, he stood with a cigar in one hand and a croissant mounded with rare roast beef in the other. His expression couldn't have been described as content, but it was darned close to it.

Molly slipped away from Michael's side while he continued to cross-examine Harley Newcombe. She approached the robust philanthropist, whose old family money came from paper goods or adhesive bandages or a combination of all those indispensable items that survived economic blips, recessions, and even the occasional full-blown depression. His bushy black brows, which almost met in the middle above dark, piercing eyes, rose slightly at her intrusion.

"You after my money, too?" he groused.

A puff of tobacco smoke hit Molly square in the face. She barely resisted the urge to snatch the offending cigar out of his hand and stomp on it. She settled for saying, "You don't have enough to make me put up with your smoking."

A chuckle rumbled through him. He tapped off the embers and put the cigar aside. "You're a sassy little thing. I like that. Half the people in this place are scared to death of me.''

"That's because they want something from you and I don't.''

"You sure about that?''

"Absolutely.''

"Not even a hint about the way Tessa and I have been fussing and feuding for the past couple of years?''

Molly caught the unexpectedly mischievous twinkle in his eyes and grinned. She had a hunch she could get to like Jason Jeffries. She hoped like hell he wasn't the murderer. "Okay. You caught me," she admitted. "I would like to know more about that.''

"You interested just for the sake of gossip or you have a better reason?''

"I'm interested because my friend cares about every single environmental cause that stands to benefit from tonight's event and this murder could put her and her causes in jeopardy.''

"Loyalty, huh? Can't remember the last time I saw much evidence of that in this crowd," he said, echoing Harley Newcombe's opinion. "Most of 'em would sooner stab each other in the back than lend a helping hand.''

Even though she'd heard the complaint before and seen evidence of it herself, she didn't want to believe it. She wanted to believe that ev-

28

eryone was like Liza, who was totally committed and honestly believed it was her obligation to make the world a better place. Surely others who signed up for one of these charitable boards or committees felt the same way.

"Don't you think you're just a little bit cynical?" she said hopefully.

"A little bit? Hell, girl, I've lived a long time and I'm damned cynical. I have cause to be. Human beings have a tremendous capacity for hurting their fellow man, to say nothing of God's creatures. What they'll do to them is a crying shame."

"Didn't you and Tessa agree on that much at least?"

"Sure we did."

"Then what was the problem between you?"

"To understand the answer to that you'd have to go back thirty years or so, before your time, I suspect."

"Barely," Molly admitted with great reluctance. Her thirtieth birthday was less than two weeks away. She was not looking forward to it. Too much of her life was not the way she'd planned for it to be. "So what happened between you and Tessa thirty years ago?"

Jason Jeffries knew how to draw out suspense. He ate the last bite of his sandwich, wiped his pudgy fingers delicately on a pristine white handkerchief he drew from an inner pocket, folded it neatly, and put it away. Then, with an air of nonchalance that had Molly gnashing her teeth, he took her arm and led her deep into the shadows on the terrace.

Considering that Jason Jeffries might very well be a suspect in Tessa's murder, Molly knew she should have been terrified at being lured farther away from the crowd. A distant rumble of thunder and the dimming of the outdoor lights emphasized the warning. Instead of being frightened, however, her anticipation soared the way it always did when she knew some major clue was about to be revealed.

Only when they were alone and the bay was spread before them did he speak.

With his unflinching gaze pinned directly on her, he said quietly, "It all started when I married the damned woman."

CHAPTER
THREE

Discovering that Tessa Lafferty and Jason Jeffries had been married was like discovering that a tiger and a bumble bee were distant cousins. Molly spent a full two minutes processing the image of the unlikely relationship before she managed a coherent word.

"What?" Okay, it was weak, but it was the best she could do given the astonishing nature of his revelation.

Jason Jeffries grinned. "Hadn't heard that one, had you? Not many people have. Tessa liked to keep it a deep, dark secret. She hated failure, and believe me, our marriage was a doozy of a disaster from the first day."

"Do the police know?"

"They do. Why would I try to hide a thing

like that? Folks may not recall much about it, but there are records down at the courthouse." He waggled a finger under her nose. "Let this be a lesson to you. There's no use denying the truth. It'll just backfire on you, when you least expect it."

"But revealing it might move your name to the top of the list of suspects and distract the police from the real killer."

He beamed at her. "Thank you for assuming that I'm innocent. You're a good judge of character. I didn't do it. If I was planning to murder Tessa, I would have done it years ago when I discovered she loved money, hated sex, and used men the way folks with a cold use tissues. Took me less than a month to catch on. We were divorced six miserable months later. Can't for the life of me figure out how a man as smart as Roger Lafferty got himself married to her."

"You did."

"But I was young and naive at the time and I didn't stay married to her the way Roger has."

"You must have been . . ."

He scowled at her with feigned ferocity. "Don't waste your energy trying to count backwards, young lady. I was forty-two. Should have known better, but Tessa was a decade or more younger and she was a beauty. That blond hair of hers was natural then, and just like silk. She had a figure that would stop men dead in their tracks.

She had a way of making a man do things that were downright foolish.''

"Then don't you suppose that's the same effect she had on Roger?"

"By the time they met, she'd been around the block a few times. The word was out, especially in our crowd. He ignored it all. His wife had just died. He was lonely. And Tessa took advantage.''

"But you said yourself, men in love do foolish things.''

"They do indeed,'' he agreed. "That's why I avoided another folly like that one. After Tessa, I steered clear of women with marriage on their minds. Can't trust 'em to behave the same way, once they have their hooks in you.''

"You never married again?"

"No.''

She regarded him speculatively, searching for signs of regret, some hint of sorrow over his exwife's death. "Some might think that indicates you never got over Tessa. Were you still in love with her?"

"Good lord, no!'' he said with genuine horror at the notion.

"Then why the fights?"

"She was a vain, silly woman. Lately she actually latched on to a little power, thanks to Roger's standing in the community. Power and stupidity are a dangerous combination. I warned her again and again that she didn't know what the hell she was doing. I'm on a lot of boards in this town. I know a thing or two about fund-raising and a lot about business. I got my hands on the books after a couple of these fund-raisers and threw a holy tantrum over the waste. I threatened to expose her as a fraud if she didn't start bringing the profit margin in line before we had the IRS staring over our shoulders, eyeballing every little thing, questioning our nonprofit status."

That might have been reason for Tessa to fear Jason, perhaps even a motive for her to murder him, but Jason wasn't the one who'd been found floating in the bay.

"Did you two quarrel tonight?" Molly asked, wondering if perhaps Tessa had lured Jason to that secluded spot intending to clobber him with something, only to have the tables turned on her in a struggle. Not that there was any indication from Jason Jeffries's perfectly tailored, unmussed tuxedo that he'd struggled with anything more taxing than that oversized roast beef sandwich. Of course, to a man of his girth and height, a woman of Tessa's fragile frame would be little more than a pesky nuisance. He could probably have nabbed her by the nape of her neck and tossed her aside without even breathing hard, even if he was in lousy shape.

"Nope. No quarrel," he said.

The flat denial shattered the volatile scenario Molly was envisioning.

34

He elaborated. "Never said a word to her. I spent most of the evening talking to that perky young gal who's after my money to help save the manatees."

"Liza Hastings," Molly said, wondering how Liza would take to being described as either "perky" or a "gal." She was close to ten years older than Molly. Thanks to incredible genes and an exercise regimen that would do in Jane Fonda, she didn't look her age. However, she did not suffer sexist little euphemisms kindly. Of course, chances were good that Jason Jeffries knew that and simply refused to mend his ways to suit her.

"Liza," he said. "That's the one. Girl's got a head on her shoulders. If she'd been running this thing tonight, they'd have made a bundle."

"I suspect she'd agree with you about that."

He regarded her with renewed interest. "Is she your friend, the one you mentioned earlier?"

"Yes."

He nodded approvingly. "I like that. A couple of tough cookies. You keep in touch. Tell your friend to make her plans. Don't schedule anything before the height of the winter season, though. Might as well take all those snowbirds for all they're worth. She can send me the bills. I'll underwrite whatever she wants to put together to save the manatees. Sign up that Buffet person to help. We'll teach this town a thing or two about fund-raising."

He turned and strolled away with astonishing grace for a man of his age and size. Judging from the direction in which he went, Molly had the distinct impression Jason Jeffries intended to try to slip away from the murder scene. She warred with her conscience over whether she ought to try to prevent him from going, then decided that this would be the perfect time to turn over a new leaf. She would leave his capture in the hands of the police.

• • •

As she made her way back to the central courtyard, enclosed in recent years to protect it against the ravages of salt air and humidity, Molly toted up the suspects so far. It was an incredibly short list, and two people she happened to like were on it—Jason Jeffries and Liza. Before the evening was out she had to see to it that they were cleared or, at the very least, that the suspects list grew to a sufficient number to assure reasonable doubt.

Based on what Jeffries had told her, she wondered if Roger Lafferty was still as enamored of his wife as he had been. Perhaps his patience had been wearing thin and some incident tonight had sent him over the edge. The only way to find out would be to talk to him. Since that seemed unlikely given the cadre of protectors surrounding him, she decided a little chat with the Laffertys' closest friends would be in order. Surely Carl and

Mary Ann Willoughby were around here some-place. Hopefully, not right at Roger's side.

Molly eased around the fringes of the court-yard, hoping to spot the couple who usually cochaired every event involving the Laffertys. Instead she ran smack into Michael.

"Where the devil have you been?" he demanded.

She regarded the tense set of his jaw with some surprise. "You sound upset."

He muttered a curse in Spanish, one Molly had made it a point to look up since he used it so often. If her son had used the English version, she would have grounded him for a month. She had less say over Michael's choice of vernacular.

"Upset?" he said finally in English. "Why would I be upset, amiga? A woman was killed less than two hours ago. Someone in this crowd likely did it. And given your foolish penchant for snoop-ing—"

"Sleuthing," she corrected. It was a fine distinction, and an important one to her way of thinking.

Eyes black with anger glared back at her as Michael ran through his entire repertoire of colorful curses, at least one of which Molly suspected implored the gods to lend divine assistance. He looked as if he were just itching to shake some sense into her. Molly's chin went up.

"Don't use that sort of language around me," she said huffily, and turned on her heel.

"You don't speak Spanish," he shot back, though he looked somewhat chagrined when she peeked at him over her shoulder.

"I speak enough," she informed him.

His gaze narrowed. "Enough to carry on a conversation? Or just enough to get yourself into trouble on the street?"

"Tío Pedro says I order dinner in perfect Spanish."

"Tío Pedro would tell you that if you mangled every word. He's a gentleman."

"A gentleman who would be appalled by the language you just used around a lady."

"Okay, yes," he conceded. "I apologize. But that does not negate the stupidity of your going off alone in the dark in the midst of a murder investigation."

"I wasn't alone," she said, and recounted her conversation with Jason Jeffries. As she'd expected, the information she'd gleaned took Michael's mind off what he'd viewed as her foolish disappearance.

"By the way, I'm sorry if you were worried," she added at the end. It had been a long time since anyone had genuinely cared what happened to her.

"I was worried," he said emphatically. "You tend to think you're indomitable. It's a dangerous state of mind when you're messing with a murderer.''

Molly conceded the logic in his warning. "I know you're right. I just assume everyone will dismiss me as some naive, slightly nosy single mother and spill their guts to me without thinking anything of it.''

"They might have done that six months ago, but I suspect most of these people know all about your involvement in solving those other murder cases. They'll be on guard with you, or worse, they'll consider you an enemy who's getting too close to the truth. The good Lord may protect fools, but even He can do only so much. For your sake and the sake of your son, stay out of the investigation, Molly. I can't put it any plainer than that.''

"But Liza could need my help.''

"I still wish you'd tell me why you're so convinced she needs help.''

"I've explained that,'' she said stubbornly.

"She's openly stated that she detested the woman,'' he repeated. "Okay, then, the best way you can help Liza is by being supportive and staying alive. Meddling in the case won't do it.'' He watched closely as if to assure himself that she'd gotten the message. Finally, he nodded in satisfaction. "I want to go fill the police in on what Jason Jeffries told you.''

"He said he'd already told them.''

"And you believed him?"

"Yes."

"Molly, a man who just committed a murder might not be above a little lying."

"He didn't do it," she said staunchly. "Not any more than Liza did."

"I'm glad you're convinced, but I think I'll share the information with the police just the same. Stay put," he said when she started to wander off in the opposite direction.

She stayed where she was until he was out of sight, then set out to mingle some more. Inside. In plain view of lots of witnesses. There was no telling what she might overhear. Listening wouldn't be breaking her vow to Michael. Not exactly, anyway.

Besides, she really wanted to get a better sense of what Tessa Lafferty had been like. Clearly Liza and Jason Jeffries had pretty jaded views of the woman. Her own contact with her had been limited. Surely there were others who held more kindly memories.

Then, again, if all the rumors she'd heard over the years were true, maybe not.

CHAPTER
FOUR

Tessa Lafferty was a bitch. Everyone said so, according to Liza's frequent, biased reports over the months of planning for this gala. Everyone had a story to tell about how Tessa had slighted them, run roughshod over them, offended them, or, in some instances, even betrayed them. They discussed her lousy behavior as if tolerating it were some kind of badge of honor. Molly was surprised half the women on the committee hadn't gone out and purchased buttons declaring I SURVIVED TESSA LAFFERTY.

And yet, to Molly's amazement, they worked with her. When she'd asked why, Liza had pointed to her powerful name, her sizable bank account, and her formidable determination to get the job done. Mary Ann Willoughby had also run interference.

Despite the enjoyment her committee had once taken in ripping her to shreds, apparently things had changed now that the discovery of her body indicated some discretion was called for. As Molly circled through the rooms surrounding the courtyard on Vizcaya's lower floor—the Adam Library, the Renaissance Hall, the East Loggia, the Music Room, the Banquet Hall, and then finally the Tea Room—she was astounded at how many of these previously declared enemies suddenly adored the woman.

"So generous," said one aging dowager, who only a few weeks ago had cut Tessa dead in a Bal Harbour boutique favored by the society matrons. Word of the slight by Patrice MacDonald had spread like wildfire. Even Molly, who was not normally plugged into that particular rumor mill, had heard about the incident by nightfall. Liza's report had been especially gleeful.

"Such an organizer," commented another, who'd battled to have Tessa removed as chairwoman for one of her own pet charity functions.

"A class act. Truly a class act," noted yet another, whom Molly recognized as the wife of a man who'd just recently had a widely known, passionate fling with the ever-so-classy Tessa.

The three women managed to deliver their praise with straight faces, a feat that Molly felt was deserving of some mention. She joined them against the backdrop of a stained glass wall beyond which the lit gardens were on display. Since all that glass reminded her of a church, perhaps it would be enough to inspire a few confessions.

"I'm sure you all must be distraught," she said, lacing the observation with a heavy dose of somber sympathy that she hoped would cover her inexplicable nosiness. "I know you all traveled in the same social circle. How long have you known Tessa?"

She glanced first at Patrice MacDonald, whose platinum blond hair had been lacquered into place with sufficient spray to withstand a hurricane. Her beaded gown dipped low in front to reveal an impressive amount of cleavage. It was a daring display for someone of her age. Not even the diamond and pearl necklace at her throat could draw attention upward.

"Years," the dowager said with a frosty smile. "I recall when Tessa moved to Miami."

There was every indication from her tone that Patrice still considered Tessa to have been an interloper, even though Molly knew for a fact that Tessa's family had settled in Miami at least fifty years earlier. The two women had grown up within blocks of each other in Coral Gables, had attended the same private schools and the same coming-out parties. Their fathers had both served on the prestigious and very exclusive Orange

Bowl Committee, which only in recent years had reluctantly begun to add women and minorities to its membership.

"And you?" Molly asked Helen Whorton, who championed half a dozen causes, though she focused most of her attention on the needs of the area's major teaching hospital. "I seem to recall that you were both trying to raise money for diabetes research."

"Alzheimer's," Helen corrected tersely, her arthritic hands nervously twisting the pale mauve chiffon scarf that the designer no doubt had intended as a wrap to cover saggy older arms. Her eyebrows, which had risen after several face-lifts, gave her a perpetual air of surprise. The skin under her chin was smooth, however. She probably considered it a fair exchange.

"Wasn't there some argument?" Molly inquired with the innocence of a newborn.

"A minor disagreement," Helen murmured, glancing around with a look that a suspicious mind might have interpreted as desperate. "I really must find George. I can't imagine where he's disappeared to."

"Don't fret, dear," Patrice told her. "I'm sure he and Clark are somewhere together, probably trying to tell the police how to do their jobs."

Molly wondered if George Whorton and Patrice's escort, attorney Clark Dupree, were having any better luck at that than she usually had. Be-

fore she could become too distracted by that speculation, she took one last stab at eliciting an honest reaction from the women before one of them
wised up and told her to take a hike. She turned
to Caroline Viera, the youngest of the three and
the wife of a major banking figure. Her accep-
tance in this particular set of old Miami society
was silent testimony to her husband's command-
ing position.

"Were Tessa and Roger close friends with you
and Hernando?"

"Roger and Hernando are business associates," the petite, elegant woman, who'd recently
made an annual best-dressed list for the second
time in a row, said coolly. "I knew Tessa only by
reputation."

"You've never served on any committees with
her?" Molly asked, surprised. She'd thought committee work was a way of life in this crowd.

Caroline arched one carefully sculpted brow
disdainfully. "I have little time for committees. I
have a business of my own to run."

"Of course," Molly said at once, surprised
that she'd forgotten that Caroline Davis-Whit-
comb had built an impressive list of professional
credentials before marrying Hernando. A few de-
cades ago, she would have given all that up after
the wedding, using her skills when called upon on
a slew of committees. Obviously, however, Davis-

Whitcomb Inc. had continued to thrive after the marriage and Caroline was proud of the fact.

"Public relations, isn't it?" Molly added.

"Advertising and public relations."

"Isn't tonight's event one of those you handled on a *pro bono* basis?" Molly asked. It was all beginning to come back to her now. Liza actually had described the elaborate arrangements necessary to keep Caroline and Tessa apart yet focused on the same goal.

Caroline hadn't built a million-dollar PR business by not knowing her stuff. In her best public relations manner, she shrugged indifferently. "At my husband's request, I believe I did have someone assigned to help out. The firm often does that for worthy causes."

Before Molly could even formulate another question, Patrice linked her arm through Helen's. "Darlings, I believe I see George and Clark going into the courtyard. Surely Hernando cannot be far away. Shall we go see what they've learned?"

The three brushed past Molly in a whisper of chiffon without so much as a farewell. She could understand their rush. What puzzled her more was why none of the three had asked a single question about her discovery of the body, a fact that had surely made the rounds by now. Unless, of course, one or all of them knew everything there was to know about exactly how Tessa Lafferty had ended up in Biscayne Bay and didn't much care about Molly's own role in tonight's sad events.

Molly walked outside where it was quieter. She was still toying with the concept of one of the three being a murderer, bringing her list of suspects up to a more respectable five, when Liza found her. She looked absolutely spent, as if every ounce of her normal vivaciousness had drained away.

"This could very well be the worst night of my life," she announced wearily, rather than with her more typical dramatic flourish. Without regard for propriety, she hiked her narrow skirt up well above her knees to permit more freedom of movement and paced in an agitated circle.

"Liza, you'll have to pay extra to replace the lawn, if you keep that up," Molly said finally, regarding her friend closely for some hint that it was guilt, not simply distress, that had her in such a state.

Liza gave her a rueful smile, stopped in place, and allowed her skirt to slither back down over slender hips to where it belonged. She ran her fingers through her cropped hair, currently darkened to a shade of auburn that wouldn't clash with her dress. The gesture left the modified flattop in erratic spikes. "How could this happen, tonight of all nights?" she demanded, as if she expected Molly to have an answer.

"If a woman's going to be murdered, it might as well be someplace with a whole houseful of suspects," Molly retorted.

Liza glared at her. "Are you implying that this was premeditated?" she said sharply.

"I'm not implying anything," Molly soothed, her concern growing over Liza's oddly defensive behavior and that unexplained absence. "I'm just saying that there are five hundred people here, any one of whom had the opportunity to kill Tessa. It sure as hell beats shooting her in her own living room with that private security guard you told me they have on duty standing at the front gate. Why did Roger hire that guard anyway? You'd think the Dobermans would be message enough for any burglar contemplating a break-in."

"The neighborhood's changing."

"Are we talking about Coral Gables, that bastion of the rich?"

"There are old-money rich and then there are the other kind," Liza pointed out. The tension in her voice seemed to be easing, as if she felt she were on safer turf. "Tessa was convinced that half the houses in their neighborhood belong to big-time drug dealers now. Roger wanted to make sure some disgruntled druggie didn't come barging into their house by mistake."

"Are you sure there hadn't been threats against him or Tessa?"

Liza looked startled by the implication. "I'm not sure of it, no," she said slowly. "But why would either of them be in any kind of danger?"

"Obviously one of them was."

"Unless Tessa's death was an accident," Liza said hopefully. "Maybe she stumbled, hit her head, fell into the bay, and drowned. You know how high her heels were. I'm surprised she didn't fall flat on her face every time she tried to take a step on this grass."

"She was found in the water next to one of the most deserted sections of the estate," Molly reminded her. "Why would she have gone all the way over there alone? Surely you don't suppose she needed a respite from all of the adulation being heaped on her as a result of tonight's success?"

"I have no idea, but that brings up something else," Liza said, a speculative gleam in her eyes that should have made Molly instantly suspicious. "What were you and the hunk doing over there?"

Molly refused to feed Liza's insatiable need to meddle in her love life, or lack thereof. "Having a quiet glass of champagne."

"Right," Liza said skeptically.

"That's all," Molly insisted, though there was no mistaking the defensive note in her own voice now. She would not admit, even to her very best friend, that she had followed Michael to that isolated spot in the wild hope of sharing a steamy romantic interlude.

Perhaps, she thought suddenly, Tessa had indulged in a similar fantasy. Not with Michael, of course, but some other guest?

"Liza, was Tessa still having an affair with Hernando?"

"Hernando? Surely by now he had wised up."

"Then someone else?"

Liza regarded her as if the very idea of Tessa as a femme fatale were ludicrous. "I'm surprised her own husband shared a house with her. I can't imagine some other man finding her passionately exciting. That thing with Hernando must have been a fluke."

"You're prejudiced," Molly pointed out, not quite ready to divulge what Jason Jeffries had told her about Tessa's penchant for using and discarding men. "Think about some of the men involved with this particular fund-raising project. How did she get along with them? Did she flirt, bat those false eyelashes of hers? Did they come on to her?"

Liza's expression turned thoughtful. "I suppose there was a certain chemistry between her and old man Jeffries. I always thought it was because they were highly competitive, but maybe there was an edge of passion to the outward expressions of hatred and distrust."

"Maybe once upon a time," Molly confided.

"He just told me he and Tessa used to be married."

"Now there's a picture," Liza said, her expression far less astonished than Molly might have liked. "I thought he had better sense."

"I believe he views it as a youthful indiscretion. You weren't surprised about their marriage, were you?"

Liza actually paused to consider the question. "Now that you mention it, no. I think I'd heard it before."

"Who told you? He said Tessa liked to keep it a secret."

"Unless they were married in a wedding chapel in Vegas, divorced in the Dominican Republic, and never passed through Miami in between, it wasn't a secret," Liza said flatly. "Have the police questioned you yet?"

"Not really. I gave a statement about discovering the body to Detective Abrams when they first got here, but that may be it for me. I think Michael would prefer it if I never got within a hundred yards of the police. He suspects it will only whet my appetite for investigating the murder myself."

"Which, of course, it will," Liza observed.

Molly scowled at her. "What about you? Liza, I have to ask. Where were you earlier?"

The question seemed to take her friend by

surprise. "You mean when Tessa was killed, don't you?"

Molly winced at the look of betrayal in Liza's eyes. "Yes."

Liza sighed heavily. "I can't tell you that."

"But . . ."

"I can't."

"What if the police ask?"

"They did. I was the first one they questioned. After Roger, of course."

Molly didn't like the sound of that. "Why?"

"They didn't say, but obviously you weren't the only one wondering about where I'd been. And I suspect Roger told them that Tessa and I were at odds over the way this fund-raiser was being run."

"At odds? Isn't that a little like suggesting the troops in Vietnam were a mere military presence?"

"Whose side are you on?"

"Yours, but everyone knows you and Tessa couldn't stand each other. Roger's testimony won't be the last they hear along those lines. You said you blew up at her at the last committee meeting. I assume there were others present."

"A whole roomful," Liza admitted. "Okay, so there is a block of time I can't account for. I suppose that means I had opportunity and a possible motive, but you have to admit that makes a pretty weak case. When was the last time someone killed someone just because they were terminally dim-witted?''

Molly moaned. "Liza, you have to stop saying stuff like that.''

"Why? It's the truth. Do you know how much money that woman wasted on invitations because she just had to have one that was die-cut and em-bossed so it would make a statement? Four thou-sand dollars, that's how much. She didn't even use recycled paper, for heaven's sake. When I heard that, I hit the roof.'' She took to pacing again, her temper heating up all over again. "And I'll tell you what statement it made. It said she was more concerned with her own ridiculous image than she was about the environment. She should have been shot.''

"Liza!''

Molly's protest apparently penetrated. Liza sighed heavily. "Jesus! I know I shouldn't say stuff like that, but it makes me so furious . . .''

"How furious?'' Michael inquired lightly as he joined them.

Molly and Liza both swallowed hard, then tried to explain at once.

"Hold it! Stop!'' he said when he could fi-nally get a word in. "You don't have to convince me that the remark was entirely innocent, but you'd better be careful where else you say things like that. The detective in charge of this case is a by-the-book kind of guy. There will be a lot of pressure, given the status of those attending tonight. He is going to be very anxious to see that it's solved in a hurry."

"I tried to tell her," Molly said.

"I know. I'll shut up," Liza promised. "I just had to get that off my chest."

"In the future vent your anger in the privacy of your own home," Michael suggested mildly.

Hoping to distract him from a full-blown lecture, Molly inquired, "What's happening in there? Have the police narrowed the list of suspects down yet?"

"That's not something they're sharing with me."

"What about the cause of death?"

"I'm not on the need-to-know list for that either."

Molly glared at him. "What good is being at a murder with a policeman if he won't tell you anything?"

"Maybe next time you'd prefer to be escorted by your ex-husband. I understand he loves this sort of thing."

The dig struck home. Hal DeWitt loved being around money and power. It gave him the perfect opportunity to suck up. Molly was sure the only reason he was absent tonight was because Liza's name had been on the invitation and he'd guessed Molly would be in attendance.

"If you're going to ruin a reasonably pleasant

conversation by bringing up my ex, I think I'll take another walk around the grounds until the police want me."

To her chagrin no one tried to stop her when she strolled off in the direction of the catering tent. It was too bad, too, because she was just in time to see society caterer Neville Foster launch into a shouting match with one of the hapless servers who'd been in charge of shaving off wafer-thin slices of rare roast beef earlier in the evening.

"What do you mean it is missing?" he screamed, hands on narrow hips. "How could you be so careless, so inept?"

"It was there earlier," the man insisted stubbornly, refusing to be intimidated by Neville's outrage. "I recall lighting the candles myself."

"So you are saying that one of the guests just happened to walk off with an antique silver candlestick tucked in her purse?" the caterer inquired so sarcastically that Molly winced. "What would anyone at this affair need with such a candlestick? No doubt they own pieces three times as valuable."

Molly glanced at the other end of the buffet table where a heavy, ornate candlestick still held a softly glowing candle. She could think of one distinct reason someone might need such an object. It would make a dandy murder weapon.

CHAPTER
FIVE

The expression on Michael's face was not particularly welcoming when Molly came tearing back around to the terrace where she'd left him and Liza comparing notes on the murder.

"Where did you run off to this time?" he inquired testily.

"You won't be quite so cranky when I tell you what I discovered," Molly retorted.

"Try me."

"I've found the murder weapon. Well, I haven't found it exactly, but I know what it was."

He refused to look impressed. "Considering that no one has established that Tessa Lafferty was murdered, that's quite a feat," he said.

She decided to ignore his stubborn denial of something everyone else on the grounds accepted as true. The police were certainly treating the death as if it were a homicide, even if the word hadn't been used yet. That was enough for Molly.

"A silver candlestick is missing from the buffet table," she said, deciding no embellishment was needed. Michael would get the implication. She noted the reluctant spark of interest in his eyes with satisfaction.

"Are you trying to suggest that Tessa Lafferty went for a stroll with someone toting along a heavy candlestick?" he inquired doubtfully. "Wouldn't she have noticed?"

It was a reasonable question. Molly had already thought of it. She had an answer. "If the murderer was a woman, it could have been in her purse."

Michael cast a significant look at the tiny evening bag in her hand, then glanced at Liza. She carried no purse at all.

"Okay, yes, mine's too small," Molly conceded. "But we won't know about the others until we look."

"You're wasting your time. There's not a woman in the place carrying a purse large enough to conceal more than a tube of lipstick and maybe a solid gold compact," Liza chimed in.

"Have the two of you spent the evening checking out every woman's purse?" Molly shot back irritably. If she couldn't find a logical means for the killer to have gotten that candlestick from the buffet table to the murder site she saw her discovery's importance diminishing.

"No. I have a thing for observing likely places to conceal a murder weapon," Michael countered. "It's just one of those things cops do instinctively."

Molly caught the slip and beamed. "Then you do agree, albeit somewhat belatedly, that it was murder?"

"I agree that's one possibility," he conceded with obvious reluctance.

"That's a start," Molly said, gleefully determined to pursue what was clearly the best lead they had. "If the candlestick was the murder weapon, then maybe somebody arranged a rendezvous with Tessa, sneaked up behind her, and knocked her out. Anyone could have slipped through the shadows with that candlestick without anyone noticing. I'll bet it's at the bottom of the bay even as we speak."

"I'll mention the possibility to the investigating officer," Michael said dutifully. "Then I suggest we get out of here."

"Now? But what about the investigation?"

"It's under control without your help."

"I just meant it seems early to be releasing suspects."

"You consider yourself a suspect? I'll admit I

58

found your reluctance to dip your toes in the water a bit suspicious, but I never really considered the possibility that you might know Tessa Lafferty's body was in there.''

Molly scowled at his good-natured sarcasm. ''There are times, Michael O'Hara, when I find you incredibly irritating.''

''I know the feeling. Liza, do you want to ride home with us?''

''Shouldn't I stay?''

''If the police are through questioning you, I don't see why. They'll want a formal statement tomorrow, but tonight I think, for all intents and purposes, the party's over.''

''I suppose,'' Liza said dismally. ''Can you imagine what the coverage will be like in tomorrow's paper once the reporters get wind of this? I'm surprised the place isn't overrun already.''

''It is,'' Michael told them. ''The police are keeping them at bay. I'll see if we can't slip out to the parking lot via the south access road, rather than going through the front door. We should be able to evade the bulk of them that way.''

While he went off to have one last conversation with Detective Abrams and the other investigating officers, Molly regarded Liza with concern. ''I'm sorry I gave you such a rough time earlier, but I'm worried about you. Are you really okay?''

''Okay?'' Liza said, a hysterical note in her voice that Molly had never heard before from a woman who climbed mountains and trekked through rain forests without a qualm. "Of course I'm not okay. I might have hated Tessa but I didn't want to see her murdered and I especially didn't want her to die in the middle of a party that meant a lot to all these environmental projects she championed. Do you know what it'll be like to get someone to chair the next event after this?"

"That reminds me," Molly said, hoping to put things into perspective for Liza. The evening might have turned bleak, but the future held brighter potential. "You obviously made quite an impression on Jason Jeffries. He said he would underwrite the next fund-raiser, if you'll chair it. He suggested next winter, when Miami is packed with wealthy snowbirds. He doesn't seem worried that you'll have any problem surpassing the success of this event."

"What success?" Liza moaned. "Our profits are probably nil. The guests are all being detained as murder suspects. My best friend thinks I could be a killer. And the caterer will probably sue because his antique silver candlestick is missing. Neville charges for every damned napkin. God knows what price tag he'll put on that candlestick."

"Liza, I do not think you're a killer," Molly said indignantly, though she had to admit she could see where Liza might have gotten that idea.

"You may not *want* to think that, but you've definitely considered the possibility. You've gone into that same mother-hen mode you adopt when your son has done something wrong, but you're determined to present the best possible side of things to anyone who might attack him for it."

"I know you did not kill Tessa Lafferty," Molly said with more conviction. "But I do think that you're high on the list of suspects, especially if you refuse to explain where you disappeared to in the middle of the party. Let me help."

"I'm not worried for myself, dammit. I'm worried about what will happen to the environmental coalition I worked so damned hard to form. Now everyone will want to go back to their own narrow interests and that's no way to impact legislation."

"I don't think you need to worry about that. Not really," Molly insisted. Michael's earlier assessment had come to the same conclusion. At the time she had vehemently disagreed, but now she could see how all the attention could be turned into a public relations coup if it were managed properly. "This party will be the talk of the town tomorrow," she promised.

Liza regarded her with a wry expression. "You're certainly right about that, but it won't be the sort of talk likely to advance our cause. If the killer's goal was to divide us all, he couldn't have picked a better way to do it. No one will want to be affiliated with a coalition when its board members are being killed off."

"Not necessarily. Why don't we find Caroline Viera and get some advice on how to handle this with the press? We'll need a plan if we run into any stray reporters on the way out."

They found a stoic, somber Caroline Viera at her husband's side. Normally charming and outgoing, Hernando looked wan and troubled, either because he feared his affair with Tessa was about to become public knowledge or because he'd been the one who'd clobbered her. Molly gazed into his bleak eyes and reassessed the possibilities. Perhaps it wasn't remorse or guilt that had turned his olive complexion pasty, but sorrow. It was entirely possible that he had truly cared for Tessa more deeply than his usual quick conquests.

Since it was hardly fitting to console the bereaved married lover of the also married dead woman, especially with his wife present, Molly was at a loss. She gratefully turned her full attention to Caroline. "Could we speak to you a minute? We need your advice on something."

"Now?" Caroline asked, casting a worried look at her husband.

"Yes," Liza said, linking her arm through the woman's and drawing her away. "You're the public relations expert. How should we handle the media? Can we salvage anything from tonight's disaster?''

There was a spark of interest in Caroline's eyes as she considered the challenge. "Here's what I'd do," she said after several thoughtful moments. "I'd tell the media that Tessa's death has put the fate of all of these environmental causes in jeopardy. As tragic as her death is, we cannot allow it to signal the end to her commitment."

Molly could practically hear the closing quotation marks at the end of the statement. Caroline paused.

"One other thing," she said finally. "Try to get to Roger. See if you can convince him that in lieu of flowers a memorial fund be established for these causes in Tessa's honor. I suspect donations will pour in, out of guilt if not out of respect."

Liza looked a bit more hopeful. "Caroline, you're a genius."

"I'll bill you accordingly," she said with a faint smile that warmed her cool, classic elegance. "Liza, you're the one who ought to take over the reins of this now. I know you prefer to work behind the scenes, but you're good with people and you genuinely care. You wouldn't be in it for the glory."

"I've been trying to convince her of the same thing. She has Jason Jeffries's backing, too," Molly said.

"Good for you. He might be an old curmudgeon, but he's well connected. If you have his blessing, you can set this town on its ear. I'll do anything I can to help," Caroline said with obvious sincerity. "I don't say that lightly either. When I commit to a project, I follow through."

Liza's worried expression had slowly begun to brighten. "Thank you. I'll think about it. And thanks for the advice about the media," she said just as Michael joined them.

He pulled Molly aside. "We can get out of here. Are you two ready?"

She glanced at Liza, who was looking more exhausted and frazzled than she ever had in all the time Molly had known her. Crusades usually charged her batteries. Until the last few minutes the prospect of this one had seemed merely to drain her. Right now she was beginning to look wilted and forlorn again.

"Liza, are you ready to go?" Molly asked gently.

"I'm as ready as I'll ever be," she said.

"Just remember Caroline's advice and we'll have it made."

The three of them slipped through the doors onto the south lawn, then set out along the access road that was currently occupied by the caterer's truck and several police cars. The narrow road wound through the dense cover of banyan trees and other tropical foliage before emerging in the parking lot.

Molly was just about to celebrate their clean escape when she spotted Ted Ryan, the earnest, wily reporter from the morning paper, perched atop the hood of her convertible. Despite the formal nature of tonight's party, he was dressed as usual in faded jeans, a rumpled short-sleeved shirt, and boat shoes. No socks. Either it was his usual attire or Molly had only run into him when he'd been dragged out of bed late at night to cover a breaking story.

"I knew you'd be along sooner or later," he said cheerfully. "Hi, Molly. Hey, O'Hara. What's happening inside? My butt was getting damp from sitting alongside that fountain at the end of the walkway. They wouldn't even bring us any hors d'oeuvres out there, much less any information. I've got an hour until deadline. I'm a desperate man."

"So what else is new?" Molly said dryly.

"If you want a statement, you'll have to talk to the police, Ryan," Michael said.

"No, wait," Liza interrupted. "I'll make a statement on behalf of the committee." She proceeded to deliver Caroline's suggested comments verbatim, earning Molly's admiration and a startled look from Michael.

Ted Ryan didn't look nearly as impressed. "So what?" he said bluntly. "I need suspects. I need details. What did the body look like when it was discovered? My photographer's out there in a boat right now, trying to get close enough to the scene of the crime to get pictures. They've already carted the Lafferty broad away by now, haven't they?''

His evident disappointment grated on Molly's nerves. "Your interest in the gory details shouldn't surprise me," Molly said. "That is what you get off on, isn't it?"

"Hey, come on," he said, clearly hurt by her assessment. "I'm just trying to do a job here. You're the best sources I've got."

"In that case, you are in serious trouble, my friend," Michael informed him. "We're not feeling very talkative."

"Molly?" Ted pleaded.

"Sorry. I can't tell you any more than I have already," she said, grateful that he wasn't aware that she had actually discovered the body. If he knew that, he'd never let her alone and she was in no mood to recall the sensation of brushing up against Tessa's submerged form.

"You've told me precisely nothing," he said glumly. Then his expression brightened. "How about we trade information?"

Michael shook his head. "As innocent bystanders we don't need your information."

"Not even the fact that the Laffertys were headed for an ugly divorce?"

"That's gossip," Michael said, his expression blank. If the announcement had stirred his interest, he'd determined to keep it hidden.

Molly was less inclined to dismiss the news so readily. "Who's your source?" she asked.

"Can't reveal it," Ted said smugly.

"How nice," Michael commented dryly. "A reporter with ethics." He opened the car door for Molly and Liza. When they didn't climb in, he shrugged and walked around to the driver's side and got in himself. Just to emphasize his impatience, he started the engine.

Molly scowled at him and tried to figure out how she could wheedle more information out of Ted Ryan, while giving nothing away herself. If Tessa and Roger had been about to split up, that could have a definite bearing on the case. Since Roger was reportedly wildly in love with Tessa, it must have been her decision to walk away from the marriage.

"Who was filing for the divorce?" she asked.

"The old man."

"Roger?" Liza said, her astonished tone matching Molly's reaction. "Why? I'd always heard he was nuts about her."

"He was until he found her in bed with one of his best friends."

"Hernando Viera," Molly guessed.

"Who?" the reporter said blankly. "That's not the name I was given."

"Who then?"

"Dupree. You know him?"

"Clark Dupree, one of the city's most prominent development attorneys," Molly said, barely hiding her astonishment. Aside from being Roger Lafferty's best friend, he was also Patrice Mac-Donald's regular escort. That could certainly explain why she'd cut Tessa dead in that Bal Harbour boutique. It might also explain why she might want to murder her.

CHAPTER
SIX

Clark Dupree and Tessa Lafferty. Now there truly was a picture, Molly thought, exchanging a startled glance with Liza. The dapper, slick, courtroom savior of more than one major South Florida development and the woman who professed to be dedicated to saving the environment from the encroachment of just such developers.

Admittedly Tessa was no Marjorie Stoneman Douglas, the well-known, feisty environmentalist, who had been an outspoken proponent of preserving the Everglades well past her hundredth birthday. But Tessa had been widely regarded as antidevelopment. Obviously her ethics, such as they were, had never carried over into her bedroom, something that probably should have been clear from the first indication that she had affairs the way some women changed hairstyles.

"No comment?" Ted prodded, obviously pleased that his revelation had rendered them speechless.

"What's to say?" Molly said discreetly. "Do you think that has some bearing on the case?"

"Roger Lafferty was here tonight, right?" the reporter said. "With his wife?"

"Yes. What's your point?" she responded, being deliberately blank in the hope that Ted Ryan would spill more valuable information.

"So was Clark Dupree."

"With Patrice MacDonald," Liza reminded them.

"If you ask me, that raises all sorts of possibilities," the reporter said. Then, as if he were expounding on a Ph.D. dissertation thesis, he added, "Jealousy always tops the list of motives in cases like this. We've got triangles all over the place."

"Then I suggest you share your insights about the geometric arrangement of the suspects with the investigating officers," Michael said stiffly. He glared at Molly and Liza. "Are you two coming or not?"

"We're coming," Molly said, defeated. Michael wasn't about to let them trek back inside for more sleuthing. They might as well go on home and compare notes. Maybe one of them had noticed something that would yield a clue when added to what the others had seen.

Ted Ryan sidled closer to Molly and edged her away from the car. "I'll call you later, okay?" he said in an undertone not meant to be overheard.

Something in his voice set off warning bells inside her. "What for?"

"So we can talk without the cop listening to every little word." He gave her a conspiratorial little smile that she belatedly realized was meant to make her heart flip over. Instead her stomach turned. Surely he wasn't flirting with her.

"Mr. Ryan . . ."

"Ted."

"*Mr. Ryan*, I really don't have anything more to say," Molly said dutifully.

It was one thing to snoop around herself. It was quite another to share her observations with the media. Michael had been right about that much at least. That really would be asking for trouble with her boss and her ex-husband. The fewer times her name was mentioned by the media, the better they both liked it. It had appeared all too often in recent months and usually in connection with messy murder cases just like this one. It was past time for her to start maintaining a very low profile. Vince had already been pressed to fire her, twice in fact. He'd held out so far, but she couldn't count on that happening again.

Engaging in some fast talking, she did her best to discourage Ted Ryan from calling. Unfortunately, judging from his expression and his persistent nature, it was unlikely to do any good.

"What time is he calling?" Michael inquired when they were finally on their way home.

"Who?"

"The young stud."

Molly regarded him in astonishment. "Ted Ryan? A stud?"

"The man has the hots for you."

She laughed aloud at the mere idea of that, then wondered if that hadn't explained the way he'd made her feel, that hint of flirtatiousness she'd caught in his voice. "Please," she protested, though not as vehemently as she might have moments earlier. "He's barely into his twenties."

"And you aren't out of your twenties. I'm telling you he's got a thing for you. I could see that last time we bumped into him during the Miami Beach investigation."

"The only thing Ted Ryan has the hots for is a good story. He's very ambitious and he figures I might know something that will enhance his position at the paper."

"Oh, I don't doubt he's after your mind, but believe me, he hasn't missed an opportunity to survey your body as well. Thoroughly, I might add." His scowl grew more ferocious. "Top to bottom. And back again."

"I get the picture," Molly mumbled.

"You sound miffed, Detective," Liza observed from the backseat. She sounded downright delighted by it, too.

Molly regarded the pair of them as if they'd both gone around the bend. The possibility that Michael O'Hara might be jealous was almost as ludicrous as the thought of Ted Ryan being genuinely infatuated with her.

She was so caught up in that particular scenario, she completely missed the opportunity to spend a couple of hours comparing notes with Liza and Michael. He parked her car, walked them to the doors of their neighboring apartments, then departed with barely a good night, still clearly disgruntled by the whole episode with Ted Ryan. Molly stood staring after him in astonishment.

Liza slipped inside her own condo, muttered something about exhaustion, and shut the door. Molly was left standing in the hall, wide awake, with not a single soul to talk to.

"It would serve you both right if I did call Ted Ryan," she grumbled as she slammed her door behind her.

* * *

"Brian, why don't we go to Vizcaya today," Molly suggested the next morning the minute her son walked in the door after his overnight visit with his friend Kevin. She winced at his choice of attire, a clashing combination of red and hot pink with some turquoise thrown in. She probably should have been grateful that his socks at least matched. Hell, she thought, she ought to be thankful he'd even remembered socks. She wondered if she dared to hope that he'd taken his toothbrush.

"How come you want to go there?" he asked.

"I'm a mother. Do I have to have a reason?" she responded, because to be perfectly honest, she didn't have one.

Though she'd thought about it all night, she couldn't explain rationally exactly why she felt this compulsion to follow through on Tessa's murder. Part of it had to do with friendship and protecting Liza, though her intrepid friend was certainly more than capable of standing up for herself.

Maybe some of it had to do with the sense of satisfaction she'd felt when she'd played a small role in solving those previous cases.

Maybe it even had to do with her approaching birthday and her vague need to feel that she was finally making something of her life, rather than just surviving.

Hell, maybe she was still trying to prove to Hal DeWitt that the approval he'd always withheld didn't matter anymore because she finally approved of her own worth. The first time she'd felt that way about herself had been when Michael O'Hara had really listened to her insights during his investigation of the murder of her condo president. She never wanted to lose that feeling of accomplishment and self-respect again.

Of course, there was also the undeniable curiosity factor, she admitted ruefully as she awaited Brian's response. She liked digging for clues the way some people liked sifting through rubble for artifacts from another era.

"What do I want to look at an old house for?" Brian grumbled finally. "I wanted to go swimming."

Since telling him a visit to Vizcaya would be educational was likely to be regarded as only one step above eating broccoli, Molly hit on the one thing she knew would fascinate him. It was a low tactic, but guaranteed to work.

"Someone died there last night," she said casually. "During the party."

His eyes immediately widened with excitement. "At the party? Wow! Did you see him? What happened? Did he fall into the buffet table or something?"

"Actually, she fell into the bay."

"Did a shark get her?" he asked with ghoulish enthusiasm.

"No, a shark did not get her."

He looked disappointed. "Will we get to see her if we go?"

"No. They took her away last night."

His interest began to flag. "Then why—"

"We might be able to find clues that will help the police figure out what happened."

He regarded her worriedly. "I thought Michael didn't want you doing stuff like that anymore."

Ever since he'd joined Michael's soccer team, the little traitor thought Michael had hung the moon. When it came to choosing sides, she didn't stand a chance. "I'm sure he'd think this was okay. It's not like I'll be questioning suspects or anything. Do you want to come or not?" she asked, losing patience. "You can stay here and do your homework, if you'd rather."

"I'll go," he said hurriedly. "Let me put my stuff away."

Molly paced impatiently as she waited for Brian to drop his pajamas and video games off in his room. Since that normally consisted of heaving the overnight bag into the middle of the floor, where it would rest until she picked it up, she couldn't imagine what was taking him so long.

Halfway to his room to check on him, she heard his voice. It was hushed and filled with anxiety. As she turned the knob on his door, he said a quick good bye and hung up in an obvious rush. By the time she had the door open, there was no mistaking his guilty expression.

"Who was that on the phone?" she asked suspiciously.

"Just a friend."

"Does this friend have a name?"

He rolled his eyes. "Of course he has a name, Mom."

"Care to share it with me?"

He considered the request, then shook his head. "Nah."

"Brian!"

"Don't I get any privacy around here?" he muttered in disgust.

Since privacy was a big theme with the two of them these days, Molly found herself neatly caught between a rock and a hard place. "Okay," she said finally, "but if I find out that the person on the other end of that line was Michael O'Hara, somebody around here is going to pay big time for tattling."

Brian met her gaze evenly in a look he'd obviously perfected since knowing the detective. It was even more disconcerting delivered by her son. Maybe she should have told him this tour of Vizcaya was educational and hoped for the best. The truth was, though, that she hadn't wanted to risk his saying no. She wanted company as she wandered those grounds again, even in broad daylight. She didn't expect to encounter any danger with police camped out there, but Brian's cheerful presence might counteract the gloom.

Based on that suspicious phone call, Molly was not all that surprised to find Michael waiting for them at the ticket booth at the entrance gate to the estate. He'd managed to time his arrival perfectly. If she'd noticed him there when she'd driven past on her way to the parking lot, she'd have kept right on going. She directed a sour look at her son.

"I had to tell him, Mom. He and I have a deal. He thinks you're too impet . . . impet . . . something."

"Impetuous," Michael said for himself, ruffling Brian's hair affectionately. His gaze was pinned on Molly, though. "Mind telling me what brought you by here this morning?"

"I don't suppose you'd buy a story about Brian needing to tour the place for a school project."

"Oh, I'd buy it," he said agreeably. "But it does differ somewhat from his version."

"You really didn't need to come running all the way over here. How dangerous could it be to take a guided tour?"

"No tours," he said, pointing to a sign on the ticket booth that she hadn't noticed earlier. "It's a crime scene, remember? The police don't want a lot of people trampling on potential evidence."

"Oh."

He slid his hands into the back pockets of his jeans and rocked back on his heels. "Okay, Molly,

78

out with it. Why did you come back? It's usually the murderer who returns to the scene of the crime. Since you weren't out of my sight until after Tessa's body was found, I think we can rule that out."

Molly considered skirting the truth yet again with some song and dance about simply wanting to walk the grounds, but it was pointless. Besides, with the gates closed to the public she couldn't even get on those grounds alone. With Michael as an ally, she had a shot at checking out the theory that had come to her in the middle of the night.

"Have the police found the murder weapon?" she asked.

"If you're talking about the silver candlestick, they hadn't when we left here last night. I haven't bothered Detective Abrams this morning. I'm sure he has enough theories of his own to check out without dealing with advice from me."

Molly ignored the implied reprimand. "I can think of two places it might be. They're so obvious, no one would ever think of looking there."

"You don't give the police much credit for clarity of thought, do you?"

"Do you honestly want me to answer that?"

"I guess not," he told her. "Okay. Where did the murderer dispose of the weapon?"

"You have to promise to let me check it out with you," she bargained.

"Molly!"

"Promise. This is my theory, remember."

"Okay, fine," he muttered with a resigned shrug. "Just spit it out."

"The pantry. I'll bet there are other candlesticks stored in there. No one would notice if the caterer's was just stuck in the middle, right?"

"It's possible," he agreed thoughtfully. "What's the other alternative?"

"The catering truck. Neville saw the candlestick was missing from the buffet table. We don't know if he ever searched for it later on the truck. It would have been easy for the killer to steal the candlestick, clobber Tessa, then slip into the catering truck and put it back with the other supplies."

"You could be right."

"Does that mean we can go look?"

"It means we can tell the officer on duty here and maybe he'll agree to let us go along on a search."

"Do you ever do anything that isn't entirely by the book?" Molly inquired grumpily.

"Plenty, according to my superiors."

"Then why are you so stiff-necked with me?"

"For one thing you're a—"

"Don't you dare make some sexist comment."

"I intended to point out that you are a civilian."

"Oh," she said, somewhat pacified. Then she

was struck by a distressing possibility. "You don't suppose they let the catering truck leave last night?"

"I doubt it, especially when they heard about the missing candlestick. I'm sure they'd want to take another look through everything in daylight before releasing anything that was on the grounds last night."

Apparently Michael was particularly persuasive with the duty officer. After a minimum of badge flashing and backslapping, he allowed them access to the pantry, sticking close by to assure they didn't disturb any evidence or make off with any of the museum's valuables. His presence hardly mattered since there was no sign of the missing candlestick amid the supplies stored in the room's cabinets.

Molly barely hid her disappointment. "What about the catering truck? Is it still here?"

"Right outside, ma'am," the officer said. "I think it's locked up tight, though."

It was indeed locked, complete with a strip of crime-scene tape across the freight doors on the back.

"Now what?" Molly asked.

"Now we call Detective Abrams of the Miami Police Department and share your guesswork with him," Michael said.

"Couldn't we maybe pick the lock?"

The duty officer looked horrified. Michael

merely shook his head. "Not unless you want to spend Sunday afternoon in a cell."

"They wouldn't arrest you, if you did it," she grumbled.

"I wouldn't count on that. Come on, sweetheart. Let's go into the Grove and have brunch. Maybe we can even catch an early movie."

"Yeah!" Brian said enthusiastically, clearly bored by the lack of action here and fearing he might actually have to view the museum after all. "Can I have the biggest popcorn they've got? With butter?"

"Only if you'll share with me," Michael said. "Molly?"

"Oh, all right. If I can't solve this mystery, maybe I can figure out why men are born with absolutely no curiosity whatsoever. The bookstore at Cocowalk probably has a whole section of books on that topic alone."

"All written by frustrated women, no doubt," Michael countered.

"Exactly," she agreed. "No man would even be curious enough to try to figure it out."

"Are you guys going to stand around arguing all day?" Brian demanded finally. "I'm starved."

"You're always starved," Molly retorted.

Michael rested his hand on Brian's head. "Just another one of those idiosyncrasies we men share, right, kid?"

"Right," Brian said.

Molly wondered, not for the first time, why the Cuban-American cop understood her son so much better than the Harvard-educated lawyer who'd actually fathered him. The easy rapport between Michael and Brian was just one of the things that made him dangerously seductive to her. It would be very easy to fall for a man who was as easy with kids as Michael was, while at the same time exuding enough sex appeal to stir the most jaded female senses. When his hand moved from Brian's head to her hip, she stopped thinking about anything of substance at all.

In fact, Molly decided eventually, it would probably take something of the magnitude of another murder to drag her attention away from the deliciously wicked way that faintly intimate gesture made her feel.

CHAPTER
SEVEN

Obviously, she'd tempted the fates once too often just by thinking that another murder might be the only adequate distraction, Molly realized on Monday morning. Her contemplation of a tedious new work week was interrupted first thing by the one other matter guaranteed to drag her thoughts away from Michael O'Hara, whose unexpected hint of jealousy on Saturday and whose attentiveness on Sunday had tantalized her all night long.

"Your ex is on line one," Jeannette said as she punched the hold button on the office phone. She rolled her eyes, indicating that Molly's ex-husband was probably in one of his surlier moods.

Molly suspected an already lousy morning was

about to get a thousand times worse. She groaned at the prospect of dealing with Hal DeWitt, who was no doubt in the mood to pick a fight after reading the morning paper and its enthusiastic reporting of one more body. Seeing his ex-wife's name in print was the only reason he ever called her at work.

"I could tell him you are out, yes?" the Haitian clerk offered, her soft, lilting voice laced with sympathy.

Molly considered the offer, then shook her head. "No. I'll just have to deal with him sooner or later anyway. I might as well get it over with." Reluctantly, she picked up the receiver and injected a note of cheerfulness into her voice, hoping to catch him off guard. "Hi. What's up?"

"As if you didn't know," Hal grumbled. "You were there when Tessa was killed on Saturday, weren't you? Right in the middle of things . . . again."

"It was in the paper that I discovered her body," she said with exaggerated patience, regretting deeply that Ted Ryan had somehow discovered that after all. "Did you expect me to deny it?"

"I don't know what to expect from you anymore."

His exasperated, aggrieved tone had her twisting the phone cord into a knot. It took everything in her to keep from snapping back with some sharp retort that would only add to his self-righteous annoyance. How had their once-happy relationship deteriorated to this ongoing stream of petty arguments?

"What's your point?" she said finally.

He drew in a deep breath. "Things cannot continue like this," he said flatly. "I won't allow it."

Hal's unusually calm tone sent shivers down Molly's back. She'd learned how to deal with his sarcasm. She could even defuse his anger, but this quiet finality was something else.

"What exactly is that supposed to mean?" she asked equally calmly, refusing to acknowledge exactly how shaken she was by the unspoken threat in his voice.

"You're always telling me how bright you are. Figure it out," he snapped in a tone that was more in character, but no less chilling.

Before Molly could reply, he'd slammed the phone down in her ear.

"Trouble?" Jeannette asked, regarding her worriedly.

"Hal DeWitt is always trouble," Molly replied wearily. "Sometimes I am simply amazed that I was once head over heels in love with that man."

"Perhaps you still have some ambivalence in your feelings," Jeannette suggested, studying her intently.

Molly shook her head. That definitely wasn't

what worried her. All she felt most times was irritation that she continued to allow the man to get to her at all. His vague threat had probably meant nothing, she told herself finally. It was just his way of tormenting her.

And yet she couldn't get it out of her mind, not until Liza called in midafternoon. It was the first time they'd talked since late Saturday night. Molly had called her apartment several times on Sunday, but either Liza had had the phone turned off or she'd been out. It wouldn't be the first time she'd holed up, trying to get herself centered, as she explained it, whenever Molly inquired about her sudden reclusiveness. Lord knew, after the murder, getting centered was probably a very good idea. Molly wished she knew how.

"What's up?" she asked Liza now, determined not to plague her with questions it was obvious her friend didn't want to answer.

"Can you get free later this afternoon?"

"Probably. Vince is out of the office and things are slow. September's not the best time to be shooting films or commercials in Miami. There's still too much heat and rain, to say nothing of the threat of hurricanes. What do you need?"

"I want to go see Roger and I really don't want to go over there alone."

"Lafferty?" Molly said with some surprise.

"Are you sure you want to pay a condolence call?"

"You remember what Caroline advised. We need to get him to agree to set up a memorial fund. It has to be done today. The services are scheduled for the end of the week, so there's still time to get some sort of announcement of the memorial in the paper. Please, Molly. I need to take care of this and I'd really like the company."

There was no mistaking the odd note of nervousness in Liza's tone. That wasn't the clincher, though. Molly couldn't resist the opportunity to see firsthand how Roger was taking Tessa's death. "You want to meet me here or should I drive to the Lafferty house and meet you there?"

"You're on my way. I'll come by the office," Liza said hurriedly, then added as if she felt a further explanation were needed, "There's no point in taking two cars."

"I'll see you when you get here, then," Molly said, more puzzled than before by Liza's hesitancy to go to the Laffertys' alone. Why would a woman who'd stood in front of a bulldozer to stop destruction in the rain forest be afraid to pay a perfectly normal call on Roger Lafferty? Did Liza fear that Roger would publicly accuse her of the murder, for heaven's sake? If not that, what?

Coming up with no logical answers, Molly swiveled her chair around in time to catch a worried frown on Jeannette's usually impassive face.

"This is not a good idea," she said, her tone ominous.

"Oh, come on. It's just a duty call on the bereaved."

The clerk regarded her skeptically. "I read the papers, my friend. This is no ordinary situation. For all you know, this man could have killed his wife."

"We won't be alone with him, Jeannette. He'll be surrounded by friends. Besides, I can't imagine Roger Lafferty killing Tessa, much less Liza and me."

"Who knows what measures a desperate man might be driven to take."

A vague chill stole over Molly for the second time that day. "You aren't having one of those visions of yours, are you?"

"I do not have visions," Jeannette said huffily. "I am just sensitive to certain auras."

"I don't believe in all that stuff. You shouldn't either. You're an educated woman."

"It is because I am educated that I have learned to trust what I feel in my heart," she retorted, her expression quietly serene.

With her mahogany skin and regal bearing, Jeannette came across as a high priestess of some sort, one whose words of wisdom should not be taken lightly. She scared the daylights out of Vince, who was convinced she had the power to cast spells. Molly was less easily frightened, especially when one of Jeannette's feelings butted headlong into her curiosity.

"I'm going," she said firmly.

Jeannette shook her head, but said nothing more. Her visible disapproval did take some of the spirit out of the anticipated meeting, however. Molly could hardly wait to leave the film office with Liza.

Unfortunately, Liza appeared to be as unenthusiastic about going to the Lafferty house as Jeannette. She had dressed in what was, for her, a sedate outfit—black stirrup pants, a black silk tank top, and a loose-fitting jacket in black-and-white silk that floated around her. Chunky onyx and silver jewelry acquired on some Mexican adventure accented the ensemble. Her pixie face, normally animated, seemed pinched. Not even the dash of her clothes could stave off the overall impression of gloom.

As they drove to Roger's, it didn't help that dark, heavy clouds were gathering in the west, promising a typical afternoon thunderstorm. A 'gator pounder, as one local weatherman sometimes referred to the brief but violent storms. With the skies rapidly turning a gunmetal shade of gray, the winding, heavily shaded streets of old Coral Gables took on a threatening ambience. The twisted trunks of the spreading banyan trees along Coral Way added to the eerie atmosphere. If they'd been approaching a dreary castle on the coast of Cornwall, Molly couldn't have felt any more as if she'd stumbled into some gothic novel. She shivered. Obviously, Jeannette's dire warnings had thoroughly spooked her.

"Have you been to Tessa's before?" she asked Liza, hoping that conversation would dispel the odd sense of impending disaster she hadn't been able to shake all day.

"A couple of times for meetings. It's quite a place, built in the thirties and filled with tile and odd-shaped rooms. When Roger and Tessa bought it, ten years ago I think it was, they redid the interior and upgraded the kitchen to something that half the chefs in Dade County would kill to have in their restaurants. They had a major hassle when they painted the outside, though."

"Why?"

Liza grinned. "One of those typical Gables things. The painter didn't check his color chips against those the city of Coral Gables permits. He had to do the whole damned paint job over again, because the shade of paint was slightly darker than the law allows. Roger was fit to be tied, tried pulling strings at City Hall, but to no avail. Coral Gables may not be able to keep out the drug dealers, but they sure as hell can control what color paint people use."

"Wouldn't you love to meet the person in charge of enforcing the color palette?" Molly said, envisioning some poor soul creeping around at dawn matching approved colors to the newly painted exteriors of houses.

As much as they tended to ridicule the restrictions, however, there was no mistaking the effect of the watchdog effort. Even with the storm approaching, there was a quiet serenity to the Gables, a sense of stability and longevity that was lacking in most other hastily developed and haphazardly planned sections of the county.

Or there would have been if it hadn't been for those newly erected walls with their security gates surrounding half a dozen houses within a handful of blocks. The decorative wrought iron gates to the Lafferty house stood open and a circular brick driveway was crowded with cars. An unobtrusive security guard, his uniform clearly distinguishing him from the visitors, stood in the shadows partway between the front gate and the door to the house.

"Quite a crowd," Molly said, smiling at him in the hope of starting a conversation that might reveal exactly what he was doing on the premises.

He nodded, his expression unyielding. Definitely not the friendly sort, she conceded reluctantly. Maybe Liza would have better luck. She nudged her as they walked from the only available parking place at the end of the driveway.

However distracted she might otherwise be, Liza was quick to catch on to Molly's intention.

She, too, beamed at the guard. "Lucky for you the rain hasn't started, isn't it?"

The guard was neither so old nor so blind that a woman as stunning and vivacious as Liza couldn't get to him. He sucked in his substantial gut and shrugged indifferently. "When it pours, I just wait it out in my car. I can see most everything from there."

"Is there much to see?" Liza asked. "Seems to me the neighborhood ought to be pretty quiet."

"Seems that way to me, too," he confided, suddenly turning loquacious under Liza's less than subtle encouragement. "Then again, if folks didn't get paranoid, where would I be? Out of a job."

"What on earth did the Laffertys have to be paranoid about?" Liza prodded. "They were one of the nicest, most respectable couples I know. What happened to Tessa was a real tragedy. Do you think it had anything to do with whatever they were worried about?"

Molly waited to see if Liza's fishing expedition would turn up anything, but before the guard could answer, the front door opened and half a dozen people emerged, effectively destroying the moment as they went to their separate cars. The guard's expression turned stoic again, and his eyes focused on some point in the distance. Apparently he'd seen how the guards at Bucking-ham Palace did it, Molly thought.

An old black woman, her hair cut short, her uniform so starched it looked downright uncomfortable, admitted Molly and Liza and led them down the long tiled entryway toward the back of the house.

"Mr. Roger's seeing folks in the garden room," she said with old-style formality. "It's a sad time in this house, a sad time," she added with a shake of her head.

"I'm sure it is," Molly said kindly, sensing the housekeeper truly was distraught. "Have you worked for the Laffertys for a long time?"

"Worked for Miz Tessa since she was a girl. Her family hired me straight out of high school. Good people they were, too. Helped me educate my brothers and sisters. Miz Tessa had her flaws, but she did right by me. Ain't nobody going to say otherwise," she said in a combative tone.

Molly wondered who she'd heard criticizing her employer and whether the remarks had been made before or after Tessa's death. "Has someone said something unkind about Mrs. Lafferty?"

"Those reporters," she said huffily. "Looking for scandal, so they are. Asking about other men. I wouldn't tell them a thing and I know plenty, believe you me."

Molly decided she didn't want to be lumped in a class with the nosy media in the eyes of this

94

prospective fountain of information. She already had sufficient clues about Tessa's marital infidelities to keep her going for a while. "Will you stay on with Mr. Lafferty?" she asked instead.

"We ain't talked about it yet. If he wants me here, I'll stay. If not, I've got me a little place to go home to. I'm seventy years old. Might just be time I retired and set a spell. Miz Tessa, she took care of me in her will. She always promised me that. With that and the Social Security, I'll do okay."

She opened the door to the garden room. "You ladies go on in and sit with Mr. Roger now. I'll be bringing a fresh-brewed pitcher of iced tea shortly."

"Thank you," Liza told her. "What's your name?"

"I'm Josiah, ma'am, after my daddy. Miz Tessa called me Josie."

Liza patted her frail hand. "Thank you, Josie."

Molly barely noted the housekeeper's departure. She was too busy staring into the garden room, which had obviously gotten its name from the French doors across the back facing a garden lush with tropical foliage. The theme had been carried over in the white wicker furniture, which was luxuriously padded with chintz-covered cushions splashed with bouquets of pink cabbage roses.

A large, glass-topped wicker table held silver trays laden with tiny sandwiches, painstakingly cut into rounds, along with a punch bowl filled with fresh fruit, and serving plates crowded with freshly baked tarts and petits fours. The spread might have been catered, but Molly suspected Josie had spent all day Sunday lovingly preparing the refreshments for the mourners who might stop by.

As enthralled as she was with the room and the buffet, what really snagged Molly's complete attention and had her scrambling for an explanation was the unlikely trio of men who sat stiffly in a row, like some sort of tribunal waiting to hand down a judgment.

Perhaps it was no more than a fluke of available seating, but lined up side by side were Roger Lafferty, Hernando Viera, and Clark Dupree. Their presence together created something of a quandary, given what Molly knew of their respective relationships with Tessa. What would Miss Manners say under the circumstances? Molly wondered, glancing at the only other people in the room, the Willoughbys, to see how they were handling the awkward situation. There was no outward evidence that they were unnerved. Either they weren't aware of the ties each man had shared with Tessa or they traveled in more sophisticated circles than Molly. Or perhaps, given their stiff, silent demeanor, they'd simply been struck dumb by the audacity of it.

Molly finally settled for offering her condolences without looking any one of the men in the eye. Let them guess who she genuinely felt sorry for, she thought irritably. While they were doing that, she would try to figure out why they were engaged in this oddly polite charade of camaraderie.

CHAPTER
EIGHT

Roger Lafferty's dazed expression never changed as Liza and Molly recited all the appropriately sympathetic clichés. Molly couldn't help wondering if he was on medication, though she supposed it was possible he was simply in a state of shock. Everyone else seemed to be. Only Hernando Viera actually looked healthy in all that basic black mourning attire, and even he looked stunned.

In fact, the only person in the room to react visibly to their arrival was Mary Ann Willoughby, who determinedly latched on to Liza's arm and dragged her away from Roger. Molly gathered she wasn't pleased to see them. Molly traipsed after Mary Ann and Liza to be there in case tempers flared . . . or on the off chance that Mary Ann might let something interesting slip. Tessa's best friend wasn't known for censoring her tongue, despite her regular efforts to soothe feathers Tessa had ruffled with even less diplomacy.

"How dare you come here?" Mary Ann demanded in an undertone. She practically shook with indignation. Obviously she took her new role as Roger's protector quite seriously.

"I need to speak with Roger," Liza said, remaining amazingly calm in the face of the older woman's self-righteous outrage.

"Absolutely not. If you had a sensitive bone in your body, you would see that he's in no shape to speak with anyone, least of all one of Tessa's enemies."

Liza drew herself up to her full height. It was an unimpressive five feet two inches, but she managed to create an aura of a much taller woman. "I was not Tessa's enemy," she declared evenly, looking Mary Ann straight in the eye. "Even though we didn't always agree on the best methods for accomplishing our goals, we did agree on the goals."

"You tried to undermine her every chance you got. I watched you do it. Who knows what lengths you might have gone to to grab her power," Mary Ann said so viciously that Molly gasped and prepared to intercede. Liza waved her off.

Mary Ann went on, her venom unchecked.

"Now you think just because Tessa's gone and you have Jason Jeffries eating out of your hand that you'll take over. Well, believe me, it won't happen. Not over my dead body."

"Given what you apparently think I'm capable of, I'm surprised you'd plant that idea in my mind," Liza retorted.

Mary Ann's shocked, faintly dismayed expression indicated she hadn't realized the severity of the charge she'd leveled at Liza. She'd practically accused her of Tessa's murder. Her gasp drew the attention of the men, but Liza paid no attention to the sudden mild commotion. She strode across the room and took the seat next to Roger.

"I really am sorry to bother you, but I'd like to make a request."

Roger blinked several times as if trying to bring her into focus. "Now? Must it be now?"

After a slight hesitation, Liza rested her hand on his. Molly wondered about that infinitesimal delay. Liza was a toucher. Her natural inclination was to pat a cheek or a hand, to give a quick hug of reassurance. Why had she just checked that impulse with Roger? Molly had never seen anyone more in need of comforting. To her astonishment, the normally effusive Liza didn't seem willing to dispense any.

"Yes," she said in a brisk, no-nonsense tone. "It really can't wait."

He sighed heavily, the sound like a child's

round plastic inner tube deflating. "Go ahead then."

"I wondered if you would consider establishing a memorial fund in Tessa's honor, a fund that would take up where she left off in supporting environmental causes. I can't think of anything that would please her more."

Roger stared blankly, but Hernando Viera was already nodding. "That is a very thoughtful idea, Ms. Hastings," he said in English that was precise and barely accented. His mastery of his second language was an accomplishment in which he took great pride. "I could make the arrangements at the bank for you, Roger. What do you say? Tessa would like knowing that her beliefs won't die with her."

With all the attention focused on him, Roger Lafferty finally shrugged. "What does it matter? Do what you like."

"You've made the right decision," Carl Willoughby told him gently. "Tessa really would be pleased."

Even Mary Ann Willoughby gave Liza a look of grudging admiration. "Yes," she agreed. "Tessa would be pleased."

Liza nodded in satisfaction. "Actually, it was Caroline's idea. I know she'll be delighted that you all agree that it's the perfect memorial for Tessa."

The only person who had said nothing

through all of the discussion was Clark Dupree. With his mouth set in an angry line, he looked as if he wanted to squash the whole idea, but knew he didn't dare given the enthusiasm of the others in the room.

Molly couldn't resist. "What do you think, Mr. Dupree?"

His furious gaze settled on her, but his tone was temperate, the tone of a man used to masking his emotions in the courtroom. "My opinion doesn't really matter. It's Roger's decision. He must do what he thinks best."

Roger glanced at him, his expression slowly shifting from bemusement into something that might have been pure hatred. "Yes. It is my decision, isn't it?" He sat up just a little straighter. "Thank you for reminding me of that, Clark. You must go ahead with the memorial fund, Ms. Hastings. You and Hernando can work out the details."

Suddenly the air crackled with tension. It was hardly unexpected given those present, but it was as if all the pent-up emotions of the past forty-eight hours had finally been unleashed. As much as she wanted to know which one of these people was capable of killing Tessa, Molly couldn't wait to leave. Neither, apparently, could Liza.

The instant she had Roger's solid approval for the memorial, she was on her feet. Hernando Viera followed her to the front door. Molly strag-

gled along behind, just in case tempers finally
snapped in the garden room. Unfortunately, the
only voice she heard was that of Mary Ann Willoughby, who apparently didn't have sense
enough to know when to keep her mouth shut.
Three male voices all chimed in to tell her.

"I will call you later with an account number," Hernando promised Liza as Molly joined
them. "I know you and Tessa didn't always see eye
to eye, but it's a wonderful thing you are doing
for her memory."

"Hernando, you were very close to Tessa,"
Molly said in what she considered to be a master-
ful bit of understatement. "Had she been worried
about anything lately?"

He regarded her with a look of puzzlement.
"You are thinking she suspected she was about to
be murdered?" he said.

"Something like that. They did just recently
hire additional security guards here, didn't
they?"

His expression hardened. "That had nothing
to do with Tessa," he said tersely. "Now I must
get back. Ms. Hastings, I will call you."

"Why do you suppose he got all testy when I
asked about the security guard?" Molly wondered
aloud as they walked to their car. Said security
guard was nowhere in sight. Either he'd gone off
duty or he was patrolling the grounds.

"Maybe because your timing was off. Perhaps

he didn't like being reminded that all the precautions had been wasted."

"Or maybe I hit on the one thing that would help explain how Tessa ended up in Biscayne Bay on Saturday night."

"Did you see that look between Roger Lafferty and Clark Dupree?" Liza said, abruptly changing the subject. "There is definitely no love lost between the two of them."

"What do you expect? They were best friends until Clark started shacking up with Tessa. That would certainly put a strain on the relationship. I'm surprised Clark had the nerve to show up here today."

Liza shook her head. "That's precisely why I think it's something more than that. It's like neither trusts what the other one would do if left to his own devices."

"So, what do you think is behind the distrust?"

"How would I know? Clark's not the only man Tessa ever had an affair with. Hell, she'd had one with Hernando, too, and you didn't see that violent reaction between Roger and him."

"True," Molly conceded thoughtfully. "I wonder what Patrice MacDonald would have to say. She obviously knows about the affair. Do you suppose she was madly in love with Clark?"

"Patrice? I doubt it. Clark was a convenience, someone who knew all the same people and was more than willing to escort her to all the right parties."

"Then why would she cut Tessa dead in that boutique?"

"Well, I suppose there was some element of pride involved, but I still think we're missing a key ingredient."

"Like what?"

"I don't know. It probably has something to do with money. It always does." She grinned at Molly. "I saw that on TV once. *Matlock*, I think."

"I saw the same episode. Some guy kept telling him to look for the money trail or something." Molly shook her head. "I can't imagine that has anything to do with this murder, though. Everyone involved has enough money to paper their walls with it if they wanted to."

"Appearances aren't always fact. Maybe one of them didn't have nearly as much as they wanted everyone to believe. People go broke all the time, especially in this economy. A few bad investments and the whole kit and caboodle can go down the tubes."

"So how do we find out who's in financial trouble?" Molly said, shoving aside the sudden vision of Michael's reaction to his discovery that she was still trying to find out anything having to do with this case.

"I can think of one person who'd know."

"Who?"

"Jason Jeffries. He's got his finger in every financial pie in town."

"How do you suppose he'd feel about us dropping by uninvited?" Molly asked, her curiosity fully aroused. "He thinks we're a couple of tough cookies. He'd probably get a kick out of knowing that we're sleuthing."

"Unless, of course, he's the one who murdered Tessa."

Molly's eyes widened at Liza's matter-of-fact tone. "You don't believe that."

"No," Liza said thoughtfully, "I don't. But who knows what the police think, and at the moment they probably have more evidence than we do. Maybe dropping in isn't such a good idea until after we know more about the status of the investigation."

"And how do you propose we find out any more?"

"You are dating a cop," Liza reminded her.

"I think that's a pretty loose interpretation of what we do," Molly said. "Not only that, Michael is definitely not inclined to feed my insatiable appetite for clues. I say we just go see Jason. We can tell him we're there to talk about the fund-raiser."

"Wouldn't we make an appointment to do that?"

"A couple of tough cookies might not."

Liza nodded finally, glanced at the car clock,

and saw that it was barely six, not quite the end of the day for a man like Jeffries. "Let's do it," she said.

Jason Jeffries was still in his office in the penthouse suite of a Brickell Avenue high-rise. His secretary confirmed that the minute they walked through the impressive mahogany doors and stepped onto the two-inch-thick pile carpeting. She also confirmed that the odds of their seeing him without an appointment were similar to those for being granted an unscheduled audience with the Pope.

"He has an hour on the twenty-first," she told them, flipping through pages filled with precisely entered notations.

"That's two weeks from now," Molly protested.

The secretary beamed at her quick calculation. "Exactly. Shall I put you down?"

"Perhaps we could wait until after his last appointment this evening," Molly suggested, suddenly determined to see Jason Jeffries today, if she had to wait for him all night. Officious secretaries always firmed up her resolve.

"I don't believe that would be a good idea. When this appointment ends, he must rush to a benefit dinner."

"The appointment could end early."

"It's already run over by ten minutes," the secretary said, her expression disapproving.

Clearly whoever was overstaying his or her welcome would not be granted an appointment so readily the next time if Miss Eloise Parsons had anything at all to say about it.

"Miss Parsons, this really is important," Liza said in the same gently coaxing tone she used to get big bucks for her causes. "If you would just let him know we're here and let him decide."

Miss Parsons looked horrified. "I couldn't possibly interrupt him."

Molly gathered that they could spend another ten years dreaming up arguments, and the secretary would simply shoot down each and every one. She turned on her heel, walked over to the comfortably appointed reception area, and sat down. Liza followed. The secretary leapt up and came after them.

"This won't do at all," she said, thoroughly flustered by what she obviously considered outrageous audacity. "Must I call security?"

Suddenly the door to the inner sanctum burst open. "What the devil is all the commotion out here?" Jason Jeffries demanded. His gaze lit on Molly and Liza. A grin spread across his face. "You two. I might have known. Give me a minute and I'll be right with you."

Molly shot a triumphant look at Miss Parsons. The secretary returned to her desk with a sniff, then turned her back on them and began pounding on the keyboard of her computer with a touch that threatened to bounce it off her desk. The last pieces of equipment requiring a touch that firm were the old standard manual typewriters.

"I hope we never need to get past security around here again," Molly observed in a whisper. "She'll have us shot on sight."

"Not if his high holiness in there tells her otherwise. She is the sort of loyal minion who would never dream of going against her boss's wishes. She'll roll out the red carpet, even fetch us coffee, if he tells her to."

Unfortunately, the next time the door to Jason Jeffries's office opened, the two men who exited with him were all too familiar—Miami's Detective Abrams and Metro's Detective Michael O'Hara. Molly's mouth dropped open in astonishment.

"What are you doing here?" she asked before she could stop herself.

Detective Abrams apparently didn't see the need to explain his presence. He glanced at Michael, his lips quirking with amusement, nodded politely, and kept right on going. To Molly's regret, Michael showed no such inclination.

"I might ask you the same question," he said, studying her intently, then sparing a glance for Liza.

"The fund-raiser," Molly blurted. "We wanted to see Jason about the fund-raiser."

Michael glanced at the philanthropist. "You didn't mention another appointment. I'm sorry if we held you up."

Jason Jeffries smiled benignly. "These gals took me by surprise, but I never turn down the chance to chat with a couple of pretty women."

Clearly offended by the patronizing tone, Liza glared at him. He winked at her. Molly envisioned the entire fund-raiser falling apart without Jason Jeffries's backing, but before she could decide how to mediate, she heard Liza's unexpected chuckle.

"You old fraud," she accused. "You just do that to irritate me, don't you?"

He grinned back at her. "Works every time, too."

Michael took Molly's arm. "Why don't you and I let them have their meeting," he said in a tone that indicated it was an order, not a suggestion.

"Liza needs me there," she protested, then realized that for the moment her friend was perfectly capable of handling Jason Jeffries. That left her free to discover what the devil Michael O'Hara had been doing in Jason Jeffries's office. Unless he and Abrams had been there collecting for the Police Athletic League, which she seriously doubted, then her favorite Metro-Dade homicide cop had been involved in interrogating a witness in a Miami murder case.

"Oh, never mind," she said resignedly. "I'll come with you. Liza, you don't mind, do you?"

"No. You two go on ahead. I'll see you at home later."

"Stealing one of my girls," Jason Jeffries grumbled at Michael, but he winked when he said it. He turned back to Liza. "Okay, young lady, let's get cracking. I've got things to do. You need a check or something?"

Molly didn't hear Liza's response because Michael was propelling her through the door at a clip that could have earned her first place in the Miami Grand Prix. He didn't say a word as they waited for the elevator. Nor did he open his mouth as the elevator doors slid shut. The silence was beginning to get on Molly's nerves.

"Okay," she snapped finally. "Just say it."

"Say what?"

"Whatever you're going to say."

"I'm much more interested in what you have to say. You don't for a minute think I believe that hogwash about stopping by to do some planning for a fund-raiser that's not even on the calendar yet."

Molly seized the opening like a lifeline. "That's just the point. We needed to set a date. All the best dates at the hotels in town are taken early."

"Nice try, but no dice. Care to take another shot at it?"

"I'd rather hear what you were doing in Jason Jeffries's office with Detective Abrams."

"I'm sure you would," he said blandly.

She surveyed his intractable expression. "But you're not going to tell me, are you?"

"Not until you tell me what you and Liza were up to."

Molly sighed in resignation. When it came to sheer stubbornness, Michael would win out over her every time. "Okay. When we were leaving the Lafferty house . . ."

"Leaving where?" Michael said, his voice climbing ominously.

"We went to pay a condolence call, for heaven's sake. What could be more innocent than that?"

"As I recall, neither you nor Liza were overly fond of Mrs. Lafferty. Doesn't that make such a call hypocritical in the extreme?"

"I didn't ask for a lecture on manners," she snapped. "Besides, Liza needed to talk to Roger about establishing a memorial fund in Tessa's honor."

"And she required your assistance to make this request?"

"Yes." Again she was reminded of the oddity of that, but she saw no need to mention her reaction to Michael.

It was his turn to sigh. "Go on."

"Anyway, when we were leaving, we started

trying to figure out who in that crowd might be going broke.''

"Why on earth would you be wondering about that?"

"Because greed is often a motive for murder, but when everyone is rich, it gets a little trickier. We decided maybe not everyone in that room this afternoon was as rich as they'd want people to believe and we figured Jason Jeffries would know all about their finances.''

"An interesting theory," Michael admitted grudgingly. "Too bad you didn't get there in time to hear Jason Jeffries's comments on that very subject.''

"That's what you were questioning him about?"

"Exactly."

"Why you, though?"

"Abrams asked me to sit in. He had this crazy idea that since I was at that fund-raiser as a paying guest, I knew more about the players than he did. I considered explaining about Liza's strong-arm tactics, but it would have ruined my image, so I just agreed to go along.''

"You couldn't resist, could you? Tell the truth, Detective. This case got to you, didn't it?"

"Every case gets to me, Molly. I get paid to investigate my own.''

"I suppose that given the fact that this partic- ular murder involved a charitable cause, you suddenly decided you could do a little poking around for free?''

''Something like that.''

She stood on tiptoe and gave him a peck on the cheek that brought an immediate flush to his olive complexion.

''What was that for?'' he demanded.

''Because you're such a soft touch.''

Judging from his horrified expression, he didn't consider her observation as the praise she'd intended it to be. ''Don't you dare go spreading that around,'' he ordered.

''I wouldn't dream of it. It's enough that I know. Now what did Jason Jeffries tell you? You and Abrams looked pretty smug when you were coming out of that office.''

''Rumor has it that Roger Lafferty is up to his eyeballs in debt.''

''Roger?'' Molly repeated incredulously. ''Are you sure? I thought he had oodles of stock handed down through generations of Lafferty investment geniuses.''

''Maybe he did, but he's broke now, or so the rumor goes. It's also suspected that Tessa carried a very hefty insurance policy.'' He grinned at Molly's astonished expression. *''Sí, amiga.* The way it looks, that policy could be just about enough to bail him out.''

CHAPTER
NINE

The morning headline reporting that Roger Lafferty was now officially a prime suspect in Tessa's murder wasn't unexpected, but it successfully drove all remaining thoughts of her ex-husband's disturbing call out of Molly's mind. That was her first big mistake. Her second mistake was in underestimating the depth of Hal's outrage over her involvement in three murder cases in a row, or the extremes to which he might go to punish her for it.

She had tossed aside the paper and was debating the merits of corn flakes over sugar-coated cereal with Brian when the doorbell rang on Tuesday.

"I'll get it," he said, bounding away from the table like a child given a reprieve from finishing his spinach, rather than one who'd had a bowl of cereal and bananas placed in front of him.

"Who are you?" he said a moment later.

"I'd like to speak to your mother," a strange male voice responded.

Trying to imagine how the man had talked his way past the condo's security guards, Molly approached the door warily. Her first glance at the bland face, dull gray suit, and shifty, evasive gaze warned her that the unexpected visitor was not here to turn over a sweepstakes check for a million dollars. Equally uneasy, Brian hovered protectively by her side.

"Yes?" she said.

"You're Mrs. DeWitt? Mrs. Hal DeWitt?"

"I am Mrs. Molly DeWitt," she said firmly. The sudden knot forming in the pit of her stomach was a reminder that lately she regretted that she had to admit to that much. "Can I help you?"

Just like in the movies, the man whipped an official-looking envelope out of his pocket and handed it to her. He turned on his heel and fled down the hall before she could even scan the return address.

"What is it, Mom?"

With her heart suddenly thudding, Molly gave Brian a distracted glance. "Go and finish getting ready for school."

"I am ready."

"Get your books."

"I don't see why—"

"Just do it, Brian. Now!"

His expression hurt, he slunk off, leaving her with no more excuses to avoid opening the letter from Hal's attorney, a senior partner in the firm that sprawled over two entire floors of a downtown office building.

The usual salutation was followed by a terse announcement.

Given the unusual circumstances of your involvement in several murder investigations over the past several months, we feel we have no choice but to file a request with the court to review the custody arrangements for Brian Alan DeWitt. Mr. DeWitt will be asking for full custody of his son, though naturally he will be willing to permit supervised visitation.

The letter went on with legal jargon and what looked at first glance like an outline of the timetable for this action. Molly didn't read it. The first sentence had made her blood run cold. The second made it boil. She was shaking as she punched in Hal's office number, knowing he would be there even though it was barely 8:00 A.M.

"How dare you?" she demanded the instant he picked up his private line. "Have you lost your mind?"

"You got the letter."

"You're damn right I got the letter and if you want a war with me over our son, you've got it," she said, her furious words tumbling out uncensored. It was not the way to win an argument with Hal, but she was too angry to care. "I will not allow you to use this sudden, misguided concern for his welfare to snatch him away from me."

"Oh, really?" he said.

Molly ignored the sarcasm. "What exactly do you intend to do once you have him, Hal? Will you occasionally try to get home from the office before midnight to help him with his homework? Will you see to it that the maid takes him to Pizza Hut once a week? Will you hire someone to go to his soccer games in your place? Goddammit, what are you thinking of? Don't you give a damn about his feelings? He's an eight-year-old boy, not some pawn in a goddamn chess game. If you're angry with me, take it out on me, not Brian."

"I will not talk to you when you're out of control like this," he said.

Since he sounded almost satisfied by her loss of temper, she drew in a deep breath, forcing herself—somewhat belatedly—to sound every bit as cool and rational as he did. "If you think this is out of control, pal, you haven't seen anything yet. My lawyer will be in touch. I suggest you start now if you plan to manufacture a few excuses for the way you've ignored Brian for the past two years.

Believe you me, it is not something he or I have forgotten.''

She slammed the phone down so hard the table shook. It took everything in her to keep from bursting into hot, angry tears of fear and frustration.

"Mom?" Brian said, his voice tentative.

Molly drew in yet another deep breath, then slowly turned to face him, praying he hadn't heard everything. His terrified expression, freckles standing out against too pale skin, told her that he had. It nearly broke her heart.

"Dad's not going to make me go live with him, is he?"

She saw no point in avoiding the truth. He'd have to know sooner or later. "He's going to try," she admitted.

"He's tried before," Brian said. "He came after me last time and tried to talk me into going with him, remember?"

"I remember."

"Is this the same thing?"

Molly knew that this time it was no idle threat. Hal was dead serious. "No, it's not the same," she said gently, recalling Hal's halfhearted attempts at persuading Brian to choose him over her in the past. "But it won't happen, not unless it's what you want. You're old enough now that the judge will listen to you, if it comes to that."

Brian was across the room in a heartbeat. He

flung his arms around her neck and clung to her, his whole body shaking. "I won't go with him. I won't. I never want to see him again as long as I live. I hate him. I hate him." His voice trailed off in sobs.

"Oh, baby," Molly whispered, her own tears finally streaming down her face. What in God's name was wrong with Hal that he could inflict this kind of pain on their son? "You won't have to leave here. I promise."

Admittedly, her promises didn't have such a hot track record, but apparently Brian was reassured anyway. His tears finally ebbed. He slowly extricated himself from her embrace and gave her a wobbly grin. He was far calmer than her pat, clichéd words warranted.

"I don't want you to worry about this," she told him.

"I'm not worried, not anymore," he said with admirable bravado.

"Why not?" she inquired suspiciously.

"Because I have an idea that will fix everything."

"What idea?"

"If you married Michael," he said slyly, "Dad wouldn't be able to take me away, would he?"

Molly gaped at him. "Where on earth would you get an idea like that?"

"He likes you. I know he does. And he's not married. It would solve everything, right?"

120

Marriage to Michael O'Hara might solve one problem, but Molly was smart enough to know that it would only be the start of a whole slew of new ones. She could hardly explain that to an eight-year-old. "Sorry, sport," she said with some regret. "I think this is one problem we'll have to sort out on our own."

She hadn't counted on the fact that Brian was like a terrier with a bone once he'd gotten an idea into his head. When her phone rang that afternoon the minute she walked in the door from work, she was hoping it would be her attorney with news that Hal had backed down. Instead the voice that greeted her bore a faint Cuban accent and a definite hint of laughter.

"I understand we're getting married," Michael said.

"Oh, dear Lord," Molly murmured, blushing in embarrassment. "Brian called you."

"He did. He was upset, but you should be proud of him. He wasn't letting it get him down. He has a plan, a rather detailed one, in fact."

"So I've heard."

Michael's tone sobered. "I think maybe the three of us ought to have dinner tonight and talk about this."

"Michael, no. I can handle Brian."

"I was thinking less about Brian, than I was about you and your ex-husband. What are you going to do about him, Molly?"

She sighed heavily. "I've spoken with the attorney. He's trying to reason with Hal's attorney, who happens to be one of his law partners."

"I wasn't aware that attorneys ever listened to reason."

"I'm hoping for a first, for Brian's sake."

"I think you'll need a tougher strategy than that. I have to interview some witnesses in one of my cases in about an hour, but I should be out of here by seven at the latest. Why don't I pick you up? We'll go for Italian at that place in South Miami that Brian likes."

"Fine," Molly agreed because she couldn't think of one single reason not to go. If Michael wasn't terrified by Brian's marital scheme for the two of them, then it was silly to avoid him. Besides, she always thought more clearly when she talked things out with him. Maybe together they could formulate a sensible plan of action. His methodical, left-brain approach nicely complemented her own more instinctive reactions to things.

No sooner had she hung up than she heard a rap on the door, then Liza's familiar voice, followed almost immediately by the sound of the key turning in her door. She regarded her in astonishment. Liza was rarely home this early from her various fund-raising efforts all over town. She had more meetings to twist arms than half a dozen CEOs combined.

"What brings you back from the fund-raising wars at this hour?" she asked.

"I have news to report."

"Roger Lafferty is suspect number one in the murder of his wife."

Liza's face fell. "The hunk told you."

"He did, but even if he hadn't it was all over the paper this morning and on the TV and radio news all day. If you'd pay attention, you'd have known that."

"I know enough about what's going on in the world without letting the media bias me."

Molly knew it was pointless to hike down that particular conversational trail again. Liza was stalwart in her refusal to subscribe to the papers or turn on a television. Despite that, Molly was always astounded by how well informed Liza was about the things that mattered to her.

"What happened to you last night?" Molly asked instead. "I expected you to report in the minute you got home."

"Actually I went to that benefit dinner with Jason Jeffries. I was hoping to pry more information out of him."

"Information or money?"

"Both, as a matter of fact."

"Well?"

"He gave me a sizable donation."

"And?"

"He didn't tell me anything more than he

apparently told Michael and Abrams. Roger got way over his head when he tried to take over some company in California. Tessa continued to spend money like there was no tomorrow. A few weeks ago he supposedly took out a new life insurance policy on Tessa, though nobody has actually seen said policy. Suspicion is that he intended all along to use the money to put his company back on a sound financial footing before the irritated stockholders ousted him, Jason being one of said stockholders.''

"What about Ted Ryan's information that Roger planned to divorce Tessa?''

Liza shrugged. "Beats me. Either he got it wrong or that was an alternative plan, whereby he'd try to wrangle a chunk of her family money in a settlement.''

"Do you suppose Tessa had any family money left after all this time? I thought that was why she kept latching on to all these wealthy men, so she could take 'em for a bundle in alimony. If she had her own money, wouldn't that hurt her position in getting some kind of obscenely huge divorce settlement?''

"I have no idea what the workings of the court are when both parties in a marriage have money. I do know that Jason's generous alimony ended on the day she married again. He told me that last night.''

Molly considered that. "I suppose Josie might

know for sure what Tessa's financial status was. She was pretty certain that her boss had provided for her in her will."

"Wouldn't it be a kick in the pants to Roger, if all that money from the life insurance was willed to the housekeeper?"

"I doubt Roger would have paid the premium under those conditions."

"Unless he didn't know about the will. Couldn't that supersede the name on the policy?"

Molly shook her head. "I have no idea."

"I know you and your ex aren't the closest of friends, but he is an attorney. Couldn't you call him and ask?"

The morning's events came crashing back. "Absolutely not," she said so vehemently that Liza simply stared.

"What's Hal done now?" she said finally.

"He's threatening to take me back into court to ask for custody of Brian."

Liza jumped up, her expression instantly sympathetic. "Why didn't you say something when I first walked in, instead of letting me go on and on about this ridiculous murder? What can I do to help?"

"There's nothing to be done for the moment. The attorney's handling it. Brian thinks he has a solution. He's asked Michael to marry me."

"Oh, dear Lord," Liza said, then a grin spread across her face. "Did the hunk say yes?"

"We're all having dinner tonight to discuss it."

"My, my."

"Don't give me that speculative look, Liza Hastings. I am not marrying anyone just to keep custody of my son. And I seriously doubt that Michael O'Hara considers it an option either."

"Are you sure? You know how he feels about family, especially mothers and sons."

Molly knew. After he was separated from his mother and sent to the United States to live with relatives, he was practically obsessed with the subject. "He's also a cop who feels very strongly that he's a bad bet when it comes to marriage," she said. "He doesn't even have relationships."

"What about that woman he lived with, Bianca?"

"The way he tells it, she expected more than he ever intended."

"He certainly took his time extricating himself if that was the case. Ergo, they had a *relationship*."

"I think what they had was mutual lust. Until she got possessive, he probably saw no reason to back away."

Liza grinned. "Then you're in luck. That's what he has with you, too."

"Not so you'd notice," Molly countered, feel-

126

ing oddly disgruntled. She pushed aside the feeling. "This is ridiculous. Why are we discussing it?"

"Because your son has proposed in your behalf and now you two are going to have to figure out what to do about it."

"Maybe we can just sit around and figure out if Roger really killed Tessa, instead."

"If you would rather discuss murder than marriage with the hunk, you are in serious trouble," Liza observed. "I think I'll leave so you can work on your priorities before he gets here."

"Before you go, there's something I still can't get out of my mind."

"What's that?" Liza said.

"When I found Tessa's body the other night, I looked all over the place for you and I couldn't find you anywhere. Where were you?"

Liza's expression immediately shut down. "You asked me that before."

"I know, and you avoided answering me. You're doing it again. Why?"

Liza sighed and sat back down. "Because I didn't want you to get the wrong idea."

"What on earth could be worse than thinking that you might have had something to do with Tessa's murder?" Molly said incredulously. She waited anxiously while Liza apparently considered whether to answer.

Refusing to meet Molly's worried gaze, Liza

finally confessed, "I was upstairs in one of the bedrooms—the Cathay, to be precise."

Molly regarded her closely and realized it was embarrassment, rather than guilt, that had kept Liza silent. "I think I'm getting the picture," she said.

"I doubt it," Liza said ruefully. "I can't believe how naive I was. For God's sake, I have traveled around the world and back on my own. I have challenged world leaders on their environmental policies. I've even ducked out on amorous suitors in a dozen languages. And I still fell for one of the oldest lines in the book."

"Meaning?"

"One of the guests said he wanted to speak with me privately. I assumed he wanted to discuss setting up an endowment or at least increasing his already sizable donation. I suggested we take a walk around the grounds, but he insisted it would be quieter upstairs in the mansion. Who knows, maybe he'd always wanted to get it on in an elegant room done by some European artist who'd never gotten over a visit to China."

"It is a seductive room," Molly said cautiously, recalling the soft jade-and-gold decor, the drapes of fabric that provided a suggestion of a canopy for the narrow bed.

"Obviously he thought so. The minute we were inside, he was all over me. The last guy who tried to grope me with so little finesse was a college student. I was nineteen at the time.''

Molly was horrified at the thought that one of the guests at a fancy gala would attack a woman in an upstairs bedroom. "He didn't . . ." She couldn't even bring herself to phrase the entire question.

"Are you kidding? You don't think I took all those martial arts classes for nothing, do you? The second the first shock wore off, I flipped him off the bed, pinned him to the floor, and suggested that the size of his donation be tripled.''

"He agreed, naturally?"

Liza allowed herself a faint grin. "He agreed." Suddenly the grin faded. "Of course, it's possible that his check is no good.''

Molly regarded her in shocked disbelief as she realized what Liza was implying. "Roger?"

"Roger," she confirmed. "Not that I blame the poor bastard. Being married to Tessa would be enough to drive any man to extreme measures.''

Molly understood now why Liza had been so insistent that she go with her to the Lafferty house the day before. She also realized why there had been such an odd undercurrent between the two of them. "Liza, you have to tell Michael about this.''

"No way," Liza said adamantly. "I refuse to

embarrass either one of us by spreading this incident around."

"You have to," Molly insisted.

"Why?"

"Don't you see? You're Roger Lafferty's alibi."

CHAPTER
TEN

The realization that she was Roger Lafferty's alibi had obviously never occurred to Liza. It seemed to have put her into a state of shock.

"Surely, you realized if he was your alibi, then you were his?" Molly said.

"I never thought of him as mine. I would have gone to jail before I'd ever tell a soul that I was lured to a bedroom by that man."

"Don't you think you're being a little melodramatic? 'That man' is a wealthy, prominent businessman, not some creep off the streets. Besides, it wasn't as if you actually slept with him. When you realized his intentions, you put him down . . . literally."

"Maybe so, but he apparently thought I would be amenable to his advances. What does that say about the lengths to which people think I'll go in the name of environmental activism?''

Molly shook her head. ''I doubt Roger was planning to buy his way into your bed. I suspect he simply had the hots for you. He certainly wouldn't be the first man to find your combination of brains and beauty to be seductive.''

''Maybe,'' Liza said doubtfully.

''Liza, just because you are oblivious of the way men look at you, I am not. In fact, it is sometimes very difficult being your friend. We walk into a room and all male eyes focus on you. I'm just part of the scenery.''

''Obviously the hunk doesn't see it that way.''

Molly allowed herself a tiny smirk of satisfaction. ''No, he doesn't. He seems to be immune, for which I am incredibly grateful. But that's beside the point. You have to talk to him when he gets here and tell him what happened with Roger.''

''I can't.''

''Oh, for heaven's sake, do you want me to tell him? Or maybe you'd rather talk to that Miami detective, the one who probably lifts cars in his spare time to stay in shape. He certainly looks as if he'd take the news that you were withholding evidence well.''

Liza shuddered at the thought of sharing her most embarrassing moment with Detective Abrams, just as Molly had known she would.

132

"Okay, you win," she conceded with obvious reluctance. "I'll tell Michael."

His arrival, as if on cue, prevented her from changing her mind.

"Tell him," Molly prodded, the minute Michael had a beer in his hand and a comfortable spot on the sofa. Liza looked as if she preferred to wait until he'd finished the beer, maybe several beers.

"Tell me what?" he said, regarding them both suspiciously. "Don't tell me one of you is confessing to the crime."

Molly glared at him. "No."

Liza squirmed awkwardly, her expression miserable. "Look, this isn't really easy for me, but I do have a confession to make. Not about the murder exactly, but about Roger Lafferty. He couldn't have done it."

"Oh?"

His bland response got Molly's attention. She regarded him curiously.

"I was with him," Liza blurted. "I'd rather not go into the circumstances, but there is no doubt in my mind that he couldn't possibly have killed Tessa."

Molly waited again for Michael's exclamation of surprise, maybe even a curse at the loss of the number one suspect. Instead, he merely nodded. "I know."

Liza and Molly both gaped at him.

"What do you mean you know?" Molly demanded.

"Know what?" Liza said.

"I know that he dragged you off to the Cathay Bedroom in the wild hope of seducing you. I also know it didn't work."

"He told you," Liza said dully.

"After a lot of prodding. One of the other guests saw the two of you disappear into that bedroom. She rather gleefully reported that fact to Detective Abrams. He's been waiting to see how long it would take for the two of you to come clean. Roger caved in first. I'm not sure if he was more humiliated that he'd tried or that he'd failed. Anyway, he told all. Less than an hour ago, as a matter of fact. I talked with Abrams right after he left the Lafferty house."

"If somebody blabbed, why the hell didn't Abrams just ask for confirmation?" Liza grumbled.

"Because it doesn't really matter. We don't know exactly how long you were in that room or the exact time of Tessa's death. Sorry. Neither of you is out of the woods yet."

"Wait a minute," Molly protested. "We do know the time of death or pretty close to it."

Michael's gaze narrowed. "Explain."

"It was just after nine when we arrived. We saw Tessa, with Liza in fact," she said, trying to reconstruct the sequence of events. "Don't you remember? The photographer from the morning paper was taking pictures. Tessa was there, very much alive, preening for the camera in fact. Then Liza came over to talk with us. It couldn't have been more than twenty minutes after that when we got to the edge of the bay and I found the body. That makes it nine thirty, nine forty-five at the latest."

Molly shivered as she realized how little time Tessa had spent tangled in the mangrove before she'd discovered the body. Was it possible they could have saved her, if she hadn't taken time to go back to the car for that flashlight? It was not something to be dwelled upon.

"Liza, where did you go after you spoke with us? Is that when you ran into Roger?"

Liza shook her head, her expression thoughtful. "Not right away. I think there was a crisis of some sort," she said slowly. "Yes, I remember now. Neville was complaining about the champagne."

"The champagne?" Michael repeated. "What was wrong with it? It tasted great to me."

"No, no," Liza said. "The champagne was donated, but we had to pay corkage. Do you know what that is?"

Michael shook his head.

"It means we had to pay him a small fee for every bottle opened, even though he didn't supply it. It's standard with a lot of hotels and caterers when dealing with charity functions that get donated wine or champagne. Obviously, they'd rather supply it themselves at some exorbitant rate, but some will bend their rules if you pay the corkage fee.''

"Sounds like a rip-off," Michael observed, "But I get it. So what was the crisis?"

"We were supposed to have someone standing by all evening to assure that the number of bottles he said he served were actually served. Otherwise we could be overcharged in corkage. It's a pain in the neck, but we insisted."

"Trusting group, aren't you?"

"When you have to account for every penny to a coalition board the way we do, you can't afford to be sloppy."

"Okay, so this person was missing. Who was supposed to be there?"

"I'm not sure. We'd rotated the assignment so no one would have to spend all evening in the catering tent. I can't recall who was supposed to be there. I grabbed someone to fill in until the next person showed up."

"Can you find out who was missing?"

"Sure. The subcommittee chair for the catering should have a list. Patrice never lets details like this slip."

Molly was instantly alert. "Patrice MacDonald?"

Liza nodded. "Why are you looking like that?"

"Don't you see? If she was in and out of the catering tent all evening, she would have had ample opportunity to snatch that candlestick. And if she'd been assigned to that particular hour herself and disappeared . . ." She allowed her voice to trail off so they could get the implications all on their own. They didn't fail her.

"Molly, you could be right. It fits with everything we know about Clark Dupree and Tessa, the spat Patrice had with Tessa in Bal Harbour, everything," Liza enthused.

"Slow down," Michael said. "We don't have proof of anything here. We don't even know for sure that the candlestick was the murder weapon. It might not even have been stolen in the first place. Maybe it was just misplaced and this caterer got all bent out of shape for nothing. He seemed like the excitable type."

"He is that," Liza conceded.

"Call him," Molly said. "Ask him if the candlestick has turned up. Liza, you have the number, don't you?"

"Absolutely." She reached into her voluminous purse and drew out a bulging date book that contained an entire section for names and addresses, as well as business cards. It was so well organized that she found the number before Michael could even register a halfhearted protest.

Molly shot him a challenging look. "If you don't call, I will."

To her surprise, Michael nodded. "Maybe that would be better. He'd be less likely to be on guard with you or Liza. In fact, Liza ought to be the one to call. As a member of the committee, surely you would be interested in whether the candlestick had been recovered." He studied her intently. "Can you pull it off?"

"I don't see why not," she said confidently, reaching for the phone. After schmoozing with some underling, she got the caterer on the line. "Neville, darling, it's Liza Hastings. How are you?"

Molly couldn't hear his response, but judging from the way Liza was gazing heavenward, he was giving her an earful about his current travails.

"I'm so sorry," she murmured with a certain lack of sincerity. "Getting decent help is a problem. Listen, darling, the reason I called is that I need to know when you'll get that final bill to us. We want to settle all the accounts before our next board meeting so we'll know how the event did."

She nodded at his answer. "Friday is terrific. By the way, did that candlestick ever turn up? I know how valuable it was." Her expression changed to one of astonishment. "It did? When?" She glanced pointedly at Michael. "You found it in your office. How odd. How do you suppose it got there? Or was it there all along?"

138

Molly's spirits sank, but Michael was still watching Liza intently. If he could have, he would have grabbed the phone out of her hand and finished the interrogation himself. Instead, he had to rely on Liza's quick wits to get whatever answer he was after.

"Has anyone from the committee stopped by in the last couple of days?" Liza asked, earning a beaming smile of approval from Michael. "Oh, really. Patrice came by first thing Monday morning. Darling, you didn't happen to notice whether that candlestick was there before she came by, did you?"

Liza's eyes lit with excitement. "Thanks, Neville. Everything was spectacular on Saturday. You're a genius. I'll stop by for the bill on Friday."

She put the receiver back on the hook with careful deliberation, then gave them a smug look. "Bingo."

"The candlestick suddenly materialized after Patrice's visit?" Molly said.

"That's what he seems to recall. Hopefully, he won't figure out quite why I wanted to know. If he does, he's likely to call Patrice and warn her. She sends a lot of business his way. He'll warn her out of loyalty or maybe just because it seems like a great tidbit of gossip to pass on."

Michael nodded grimly. "Then I suggest we pay a visit to Mrs. MacDonald first. I'll call Abrams and tell him what's happening. Molly, is Brian around?''

"He's at the pool."

"Then get him while I call Abrams. I haven't forgotten about that talk we intended to have. We'll go on to dinner after we've stopped by Mrs. MacDonald's. Liza, are you coming?"

"I wouldn't miss it," she said, then glanced at Molly. "On second thought, if you all have things to talk about . . ."

"Come," Molly said, latching on to the excuse to avoid a conversation about marriage with a man who was being strong-armed into proposing.

Liza shook her head. "I'll take my car to Patrice's. Then you all can go on to dinner without me."

Molly decided it was pointless to argue once Liza had made up her mind and foolish to give up the opportunity to hear Michael's insights on the custody mess. "Your car or mine?" she asked Michael.

"Mine. I left it in the circle out front. The guard will have it towed if I don't move it soon."

"Nestor wouldn't dream of it," Molly told him. "He's probably out there polishing it for you as we speak. Ever since you solved the murder of our condo president, our security chief has regarded you as his idol. He told Brian that."

Michael looked embarrassed at the thought

that a former Nicaraguan freedom fighter would consider him a hero. "I'll meet you down there in five minutes. Liza, we'll see you at Mrs. MacDonald's. Wait for us to go in."

Liza snapped off a salute.

As it turned out, it hardly mattered who arrived first. Patrice MacDonald wasn't home, according to the housekeeper who answered the door. She cast a sly, approving glance at Michael. He smiled the killer-megawatt smile that encouraged confessions and probably seductions, Molly thought grumpily. At any rate it appeared to be working on the housekeeper. She was volunteering information in Spanish at a clip that was totally beyond Molly's comprehension.

"She went where?" Liza suddenly blurted, drawing a warning glance from Michael.

"What?" Molly demanded.

Michael finally thanked the disappointed housekeeper and said good night. He turned around. "It seems that Mrs. MacDonald is in Europe. Paris, possibly. Maybe Rome. Could be London."

"In other words, she's skipped the country."

"Indeed."

"That certainly puts a new wrinkle into things, doesn't it?" Molly muttered.

"It's certainly beginning to make her look guilty as hell, especially if these vague travel plans of hers were made in the past forty-eight hours or so. Any clue who her travel agent might be?''

Liza retrieved her overstuffed notebook and thumbed through it. ''Here's the woman most everyone in Coral Gables society circles uses. I can't swear that Patrice did, but it's worth a shot.''

''I don't suppose you have her home number,'' Michael said.

''Of course,'' Liza said. ''What good is a travel agent if you can't get her in the middle of the night?''

''Obviously Patrice is of the same mind,'' Molly noted as Michael dialed the number on his cellular phone. She listened intently to his conversation with the travel agent. It wasn't going nearly as well as he might have liked.

''No, ma'am,'' he said politely, but firmly. ''You don't have the same sort of privileged information situation that an attorney would have. You can make this difficult, but I will get a subpoena. Your boss might not like the fact that an employee did not cooperate with the police, especially when that fact is likely to turn up splashed all over tomorrow morning's newspaper.''

Molly grinned at the thought of Michael actually divulging information to Ted Ryan intentionally. Fortunately, it appeared it wouldn't come to that. He was murmuring approvingly at whatever the woman was telling him. ''Yes, thank you. You've been a tremendous help.''

As soon as he'd hung up, he said, "London. It was the first flight the agent could get her on Monday."

"Then it hadn't been planned."

"Nope. In fact, the poor old girl had to fly coach."

CHAPTER
ELEVEN

Molly tried to envision Patrice MacDonald murdering Tessa, then jetting off to hide out in some cottage in the Cotswolds or having afternoon tea at some swank London hotel. It was a difficult image to conjure up. However, if Patrice actually had intentionally left the rest of them to muster up alibis and undergo police interrogations, Molly could think of a few hundred people who might want to buy round-trip tickets to England themselves just so they could tell Patrice what they thought of her before dragging her back for prosecution.

"It doesn't make sense," Liza said, echoing Molly's thoughts. "Patrice doesn't strike me as the sort of woman who'd skip the country to avoid being charged with a crime. She's so arrogant, she'd be convinced she could hire a hotshot defense lawyer and beat the rap.''

"There's only one way to find out," Michael said, already punching in what Molly suspected was Detective Abrams's number.

"Will he fly over to question her?" Molly asked when he'd explained the situation to the Miami detective and hung up again.

"If he eventually has enough evidence against her, yes. If it's all circumstantial—and for the moment it is—he figures the brass will want him to wait until he digs up something more solid before going after a woman with her standing in the community."

"Like what? A witness who saw her club Tessa with that candlestick?" Molly said derisively. "We already know no one saw that."

"Do we?" Michael said.

Molly's gaze narrowed. "Is there a witness?"

"Let's just say that no one has come forward at this time. That doesn't mean that someone didn't see the murderer and Tessa together instants before the crime and just hasn't put the two things together yet. Or perhaps he or she is holding out to protect the killer."

"So we just sit around and wait?" Liza said dejectedly.

Molly shared her impatience. "Couldn't we do something in the meantime? Maybe give Patrice a call?" she suggested hopefully.

"Absolutely not," Michael said.

"But we could sound her out, see what her mood is, determine if she's on the run."

Michael grinned despite himself. "You sound like a bad TV script."

Liza scowled at him. "It is entirely possible that she simply decided to go on a shopping spree or that she hadn't had a decent scone in months. Maybe she's merely soothing her ego after the way Clark Dupree betrayed her. That sounds more like Patrice."

"Why are you making excuses for her?" Michael asked. "A few minutes ago you were ready to hang her."

"We weren't ready to hang her," Molly retorted defensively, knowing full well that they had been. They had latched on to Patrice as the killer faster than old Roger had made his unexpected moves on Liza. "We just got caught up in the way all the evidence was pointing. Now that we've had time to think it through, it doesn't make sense. I can't see a woman like Patrice clubbing Tessa over the head and shoving her into the bay to die."

"I hope you won't mind if I don't report your change of heart to Detective Abrams," Michael said.

The remark seemed a little snide to Molly. "Maybe you should. He shouldn't waste all his energy chasing the wrong suspect, while the real murderer gets away.''

While all three adults in the car scowled at each other, Brian scrambled from the back of the wagon to the front. "Are we ever gonna eat?" he inquired plaintively. "I'm starved."

"Soon," Molly murmured distractedly. "Liza, did Patrice take off like this all the time?"

"I have no idea."

Michael nodded reluctantly. "You're wondering if this is just the way she deals with any little upset in her life, by taking a European holiday?"

"Exactly. Maybe the travel agent could tell you that."

"I'll try," he said and called the woman back. He apologized for intruding again on her evening. "I just got to wondering if Mrs. MacDonald was in the habit of taking unexpected trips like this."

Apparently the answer was a terse and emphatic no.

"She's never been this impulsive, then?" he said. "Okay, thanks. By the way, what was the name of the hotel where you said she always stays in London? Got it," he said, scribbling it down. "Thanks."

He met Liza and Molly's disappointed gazes evenly. "She has never taken a vacation without meticulously planning it ahead of time. The travel agent said she was thoroughly flustered when she called Monday morning and insisted only that she be on a flight by that night. She didn't even seem to care where it took her. Nor, by the way, did she book the return flight. The ticket is open-ended.''

"Let Liza call her," Molly coaxed, more convinced than ever that Patrice hadn't fled to escape prosecution for Tessa's murder. "Patrice would stare down any judge or jury that tried to convict her. On the other hand, flight might well be the response of a woman whose pride was in tatters. Liza might be able to get her to open up. She could say she was calling about committee business that couldn't wait.'' Molly glanced at Liza. "Couldn't you even manufacture an emergency meeting of the coalition board? Patrice wouldn't miss that.''

"I could," Liza said, regarding Michael intently. "I was going to schedule one for the end of this week or the beginning of next anyway. I could tell her that, ask when would be best for her. That would tell us when she plans to be back. What do you think?''

After several moments of thoughtful deliberation, he held out the slip of paper and the cellular phone. "Give it a try."

Liza took down the name of the London hotel, but shook her head. "Not now. With the time difference it's the middle of the night. With all the traveling I do, she knows I'd know that and wouldn't risk waking her unless something dreadful had happened. We don't want her getting suspicious and running, if she is guilty."

"You're right," Michael agreed. "You'll call her first thing in the morning, then?"

"First thing, her time," Liza said. "I'm never in bed before two or three in the morning anyway. She ought to be sipping her morning tea about then."

"You'll beep me?" he said. "No matter what time it is?"

Liza grinned at him. "You'll be the first to know." She glanced at Molly. "Or at least the second."

"First," he insisted.

"You could hear the news together," she suggested with a sly wink as she slid out of the car. "Bye-bye. Enjoy your dinner."

Molly glanced at Michael to see how he was taking Liza's innuendo. His lips were twitching, as if he was trying very hard to control a grin.

"First your son, now your best friend," he said idly. "A man could begin to wonder if the whole family intends to gang up on him."

"Not mine," Molly said with absolute certainty, imagining her parents' outrage at the mere idea of her being married to a lowly cop. "They're still holding out for me to stop all this independent foolishness and go back to Hal."

Michael regarded her in astonishment. "They took his side in the divorce?"

149

"They took his side from the day I met him. In fact, that probably had a lot to do with why we got married in the first place. They were ecstatic that a man of his obvious promise and ambition wanted me." Since she couldn't hide her bitterness over that, she glanced pointedly at Brian, who was playing with one of his hand-held computer games. "Could we talk about something else, please?"

Michael reached across and squeezed her hand. The sympathetic gesture immediately brought the sting of tears to her eyes. Apparently he saw them.

"Molly?" he said gently. "You okay?"

She gave him a watery, forced smile. "Just terrific. I'll be even better once I have a plateful of pasta in front of me. Comfort food, right?"

"So they say," he said. "I always thought it was black beans and rice."

She grinned at the cultural variations between them. "In actual fact, I always reach for hot, yeasty bread. I can remember our housekeeper baking every Friday so we'd have homemade bread and rolls for the weekend. She used to let me sit in the kitchen. Later, whenever I felt down or lonely, that's where I'd go and Arnetta would pull out the flour and the yeast and start baking up a storm." It occurred to her that she wouldn't mind sitting in that kitchen right now with Arnetta mothering her.

"I'm surprised you don't bake bread yourself, then."

"I do," she surprised him by saying. Then she chuckled. "Mostly, it's inedible. Just ask Brian."

"Ask Brian what?" he chimed in from the back as they pulled into the crowded restaurant parking lot just off South Dixie Highway.

"If my homemade bread is any good."

"Yuck," he said succinctly. "But it smells pretty good."

"Talk about damning with faint praise," Molly grumbled, but her spirits were slowly improving, as if just thinking about the housekeeper who'd been her surrogate mother had calmed her fears about Hal's threats. Unfortunately, just as they were sitting down to the much delayed dinner, and just as she was pushing thoughts of her ex-husband out of her mind again, Michael brought everything back.

"Have you considered sitting down and talking with the jerk?" he asked reasonably.

Molly glanced at Brian, worried about his reaction to the start of this particular conversation. He was busy with the garlic roll he'd snatched up first thing to stave off starvation. He seemed far more interested in consuming the entire basket of rolls than in anything they might have to say.

"Wouldn't talking to DeWitt be better than a court fight?" Michael prodded.

"I don't have any idea what I could say to Hal

that I haven't said already," Molly responded. "Besides, we never talk anymore. We argue. He attacks and I respond. It escalates from there. You've seen us in action yourself."

"I've also seen you be pretty persuasive when you set your mind to it."

"I wasn't able to persuade you to help me find Tessa Lafferty's killer," she reminded him. "It took Detective Abrams to do that."

"That's different." He leaned closer and touched her cheek. "Talk to the man, Molly. You connected once. Surely neither of you has changed so much that you can't manage to see eye to eye on something as important as Brian."

Molly wondered about that. She had changed tremendously since the days when she was a naive college girl who'd tumbled head over heels in love with handsome, self-confident Hal DeWitt. He had possessed all the strength and certainty that she hadn't. It was only after she'd grown up, pretty much against his will, and discovered that she had a mind of her own that they'd begun to have problems.

"If you want her to see my dad, does that mean you and Mom aren't gonna get married?" Brian demanded indignantly once he'd polished off the entire basket of rolls, a salad, and two slices of pizza.

Molly winced at the blunt question.

"We'll talk about that another time," Michael

152

told him, apparently unflustered by Brian's enthusiasm for that particular solution. "Let's see how things go."

"You won't forget?" Brian prodded, apparently well aware of how any conversation Molly might have with his father was likely to go.

Michael met his gaze evenly, man to man. "Have you ever known me to forget a promise?"

Satisfied, Brian nodded. "Okay."

It seemed that the evening was destined to end with a lot of promises on the line. Reluctantly taking Michael's advice to heart after he'd left her to do some more soul-searching, she dialed Hal's home number.

"We need to talk," she announced without preamble. "Can you meet me in the Grove?"

To her amazement, he didn't argue. "When?"

"A half hour at Cocowalk."

"What about Brian?"

Molly resented the accusing tone of the question, but under the circumstances she supposed it was a fair one. "Liza will watch him. I'll meet you in front and we'll see which place has a quiet table."

Only when they were seated across from each other did she note the worry lines creasing his brow, the shadows beneath his clear blue eyes. He'd given up trying to disguise his receding hairline, which actually seemed sort of sexy on him.

"You look lousy," she told him.

A faint smile tugged at his lips. "Is that supposed to win me over?"

"Actually, it was an expression of concern. You look exhausted."

"I am."

"You're still working too hard."

"This isn't about work," he said. He ordered a shot of Scotch, waited for her to choose a wine, then met her gaze directly. "I don't want to be at odds with you all the time, Molly. It takes a toll."

There was a genuine weariness and regret in his tone, but she didn't trust it as anything more than a ploy to win sympathy. "Then why the hell did you start this?" she demanded, unable to keep the sudden surge of anger out of her voice.

"Because I'm genuinely worried about Brian."

She shook her head. "I don't think so. I think you're still trying to get even because I left you."

A flash of anger sparked in his eyes, then died. He sighed. "Maybe so." He sipped his drink, as if he was buying time to gather his thoughts, then leveled a look at her. "Maybe I never understood why you left. Your parents can't figure it out either. Your decision has really upset them terribly. They're still not over the divorce."

He didn't have to rub it in. She was well aware of their opinion of her actions. Unable to hide the pain she felt at discovering that he continued to have a better rapport with her parents than she did, she met his gaze. To her astonishment, she saw honest bemusement and hurt there as well. Maybe they both had suffered.

Responding to that and unable to deal with the whole sorry state of her strained relationship with her parents, she said more softly, "Let's leave my parents out of this for the moment. I never understood why you married me in the first place. Why did you, Hal, especially when it was so clear I could never live up to your expectations?"

He regarded her with evident surprise. "Is that the way it seemed to you?"

"That's the way it was," she said emphatically.

Hal looked even more startled by her adamance. "You really have changed. When we got married, I thought we shared the same goals. I thought you wanted a traditional marriage as much as I did, the kind of marriage our families had."

"Traditional how? With me sitting docilely at home, while you worked until all hours of the night? That's the kind of marriage my parents had. Yours, too, as I recall. I think if I'd heard your father refer to your mother as 'the little woman' one more time, I would have screamed. Do you have any idea how talented your mother was?"

"This isn't about my mother," he said defen-

155

sively. "You'd never expressed any interest in a career."

"Maybe because I was too young when we married to have given it much thought. Later, when I tried to talk to you about how frustrated and incomplete I felt, you refused to listen. I had a degree, Hal. I didn't go to college just to meet a man."

"You had a degree in liberal arts. What kind of job were you planning to get with that?"

"The kind of job I have now," she said, rising to his derogatory tone. "A very responsible, creative job."

He closed his eyes, stung by her attack. "Okay," he said finally. "Then you thought I was trying to smother you?"

"Maybe not intentionally, but yes."

He shook his head wearily. "All I wanted was for things to turn out the way we'd meant them to."

"And I changed the rules," she guessed, finally understanding the anger and bitterness that had eaten away at their relationship and was still at work long after the divorce.

"Yes," he admitted. "You changed the rules and I resented the hell out of you for doing that."

"Okay, that's fair enough. We both made mistakes. I can understand how angry and betrayed you must have felt, but that was between us, Hal.

We can't let it affect Brian. He doesn't deserve it."

"You can't expect me not to worry about him, dammit. He's my son."

"He's my son, too," she reminded him. "I will never, *never* allow anything to happen to him. I would die trying to protect him."

"And that's supposed to be good enough for me?" he said, his frustration evident. "Dammit, Molly, he wouldn't need protection if you'd stop getting mixed up in all these murder investigations."

"Hal, I have to stand up for what I believe in. I have to help my friends when they need me."

"That's all very noble, but at what cost? Your son's life?" he said furiously.

Up until now, Molly had kept a reasonably tight rein on her own temper, had honestly tried to understand Hal's point of view, but now she lost it. "Dammit, stop overreacting! Brian is not in any danger."

"You can't swear to that and I don't like the odds."

"Hal, please," she pleaded, seeing the tentative, newfound rapport slipping away. "Be reasonable. Drop this custody battle before it gets ugly and Brian gets hurt."

Hal shoved the rest of his drink away, then stood up and tossed several bills on the table. "I'll think about it," he said. "That's all I can promise."

He left Molly staring after him in confusion. To her surprise, she was also filled with unexpected regrets.

CHAPTER
TWELVE

Troubled by her meeting with Hal and knowing that she'd be unable to sleep, Molly decided to wait up with Liza until she could put through the call to Patrice MacDonald in London. At least it would give her something to look forward to.

As soon as Liza started for the door, Molly stopped her. "Don't go. I can use the company. It's already one thirty. You can call Patrice from here in an hour or so."

Liza regarded her worriedly. "I thought you'd be exhausted from all that confrontational stuff. Do you want to talk about what happened with Hal?"

Molly sighed heavily. "He's thinking."

"About what?"

"Whether my promises to protect Brian with my life are sufficient to overcome his concerns."

Liza's gaze narrowed. "What's this really all about, Molly? He's not just ticked off about these murder investigations, is he?"

"No, not entirely. He's still grappling with the way I've changed. He doesn't like it and he likes even less that he's unable to do anything about it. Hal was always into power and control. He has none anymore where I'm concerned, except through Brian."

"He's still in love with you," Liza said.

"No," Molly said flatly, but she had to admit she'd wondered the same thing herself. Her relations with Hal immediately following the divorce had certainly been uneasy, but he had been increasingly difficult ever since the Sunday afternoon he'd had a run-in with her in Michael's presence. When Michael had stepped in, Hal had realized that the other man was playing some sort of role in her life, as well as in Brian's. Brian had reported that his father had asked several questions about Michael after that. He had even discouraged him from playing soccer on Michael's team. He'd suggested Little League as an alternative, but hadn't offered to coach or even to attend the games.

"Yes," Liza contradicted her. "He's still in love with you. It's as plain as the nose on your face. How does that make you feel?"

Molly sighed. "Besieged," she admitted. "I don't want Hal to love me."

"Why? Because then you'd have to deal with your feelings for him?"

"I don't have any feelings for him."

"Of course you do. You loved him once. He's the father of your son. As I recall, you didn't divorce him because you hated his guts or even because he was a terrible husband. You divorced him so you could discover who you really are. Now you know. You're a competent, bright, attractive woman. You've taken care of that piece of business. Maybe it's time to reassess your feelings for your ex."

"Liza, please don't start playing amateur psychologist with me," Molly snapped impatiently.

"You're just irritated because you know I'm right."

"Just a few short hours ago, you were encouraging me to consider marrying Michael. I wish you'd make up your mind."

Liza was shaking her head before the statement was out of Molly's mouth. "No. You're the one who needs to make up her mind. Don't hide from your feelings, Molly. If Hal still means something to you, then for goodness' sake, explore it. Don't let foolish pride stand in your way. Just because you made a decision to leave him doesn't mean you can't make another one to go back again."

"And what about the feelings I have for Michael? What am I supposed to do about those?"

A grin slowly spread across Liza's face. "Now that's more like it. Do you realize that's the first time you've ever admitted you feel something for him?"

"Not so. I've admitted to lusting after him for months. I just don't know if it's ever likely to be anything more than that. I'm not sure he'd ever allow it to be anything more than that." Tired of the entire subject, she said, "Forget it. I can't talk about this anymore. Can we call Patrice yet?"

Liza glanced at her watch. "It's about eight thirty there. We might wake her, but at least it's a respectable hour."

"I want to listen to the whole conversation," Molly reminded her.

"Then go in the kitchen and pick up the extension as soon as I've finished dialing. I'll tell you when."

Molly waited by the kitchen phone for Liza's signal, then lifted the receiver. She was just in time to hear the hotel operator put the call through to Patrice's room. Since she'd chosen one of London's most expensive hotels, it seemed obvious that Patrice wasn't exactly hiding out. It was the first place anyone in her crowd would have looked for her.

"Yes, hello," Patrice said in an abrupt tone. At least she hadn't been sound asleep.

162

"Patrice, it's Liza Hastings."

There was a faint hesitation, then a more saccharine response. "Liza, how delightful to hear from you."

To Molly's ear, Patrice sounded surprised, but sincere.

"How on earth did you find me?" she asked.

"I stopped by to see you. Your housekeeper said you were on vacation," Liza said, only slightly skirting the truth. "After that, all it took was some lucky guesswork. I had no idea you were planning to go to London."

"The trip came up unexpectedly. I just felt the need to get away for a bit, have a change of scenery. You know how that is, I'm sure. London is lovely this time of year."

The last Molly had heard they were having a record-setting heat wave. Londoners were fleeing to the shore in droves.

"I'm sure all the publicity surrounding Tessa's death was hard on you," Liza said, alluding to the dead woman's alleged link with Clark Dupree, which had come out in Monday morning's paper.

"If you're referring to her affair with Clark, you needn't mince words. Clark Dupree is a weasel in more ways than one. I'm just sorry I didn't discover it sooner," she said sourly. "Have they locked him up yet?"

It was Liza's turn to hesitate. Molly suspected

163

she, too, was wondering when sexual liaisons had become illegal.

"For what?" Liza said cautiously.

"Tessa's murder, of course. Surely they've figured out by now that he did it."

"Are you certain?" Liza asked.

"Well, of course I am," she said indignantly. "Why else would I have felt the need to get away? I didn't want to sit around and have all my friends pitying me for being duped by that horrible man. I should have known that any man who is unscrupulous enough to take the side of those unconscionable developers should be avoided at all costs. All that pious talk about every defendant deserving equal protection under the law was so much hogwash to justify what he was doing."

"But you've known Clark for years."

"Obviously not as well as I thought I did," she said dryly. "Do you honestly think I would consort with a man I thought capable of murder?"

"Patrice, why do you think he did it? Do you have any proof?"

"Who else could it have been? They were having this torrid little affair, right under my nose I might add, and I was too blind to see it."

"There are some who might feel that would give you more cause to murder Tessa than it would Clark," Liza suggested mildly.

"Me?" she said indignantly. "Why on earth would anyone think I'd done it?"

"You did have that altercation with her up in Bal Harbour just a few days before."

"Oh, for heaven's sake, I refused to speak to the little tramp. I didn't pull out a gun and wave it in her face."

"What about the candlestick?"

"What candlestick? What on earth are you talking about?" Patrice said blankly.

Molly would have given anything to jump in and warn Liza that she'd already said far too much, but it was too late. Liza was going to plod through every piece of circumstantial evidence just to see how Patrice would react. If the woman was guilty, she'd be on the next plane out of London and this time she wouldn't be nearly so easy to trace. They'd be lucky if she turned up again for her own funeral.

"One of the candlesticks was missing from the buffet table," Liza was explaining despite all the warning vibes Molly was trying to send her. "There was some speculation that it might have been used as the murder weapon. It turned up in Neville's office on Monday morning. He noticed it right after you were in there."

Molly could hear Patrice's sharply drawn breath as she put all the hints together and realized what Liza was suggesting. "Dear Lord in heaven, you can't be serious. Are you saying the police think I killed that little twit?"

"It has crossed their minds," Liza conceded.

"You tell that Detective Whatever-his-name-is that I will be on the next plane back to Miami. If one word of his suspicions leak to the media in the meantime, I will have his sorry little hide hung out to dry. You might also mention to him that he ought to keep close tabs on Clark Dupree's travel plans. He's been salting money away in the Caymans for years."

With that taunt dangling before them, Molly and Liza were left holding a dead line. Molly walked back into the living room, where Liza was looking very pleased with herself.

"I told you she didn't do it," she said smugly.

"Either that or she's one hell of an actress," Molly countered. "Has it occurred to you whose hide is going to be hung out to dry if Patrice MacDonald vanishes without a trace?"

Liza looked slightly taken aback. "Molly, you heard her. She's coming back to defend herself."

"So she says. As Michael likes to point out to me with regularity, someone who's just engaged in murder is hardly likely to be above a little lying." It felt a little odd to suddenly find herself in the role of devil's advocate, Molly decided. Perhaps she ought to leave that, along with all the snide remarks, to Michael.

"Never mind," she said, noting Liza's distraught expression. "I agree with you. I think she'll be here by the end of the day if she has to charter a jet."

"Let us pray," Liza murmured fervently. "Otherwise, I'd just as soon not be around when Michael and Detective Abrams find out she's skipped again. I may be the next one to head for far-off places."

"There are other suspects," Molly pointed out. "If we turn our attention to them and hand over the killer's name, they won't have anything to complain about."

"Good thinking," Liza said, reaching for the legal pad on which she'd been writing coalition press releases while Molly was gone. "Let's get to work."

Molly groaned. "I didn't mean right now. It's the middle of the night and—unlike you—I have a job to get to first thing in the morning."

"It's almost morning now," Liza pointed out. "If you go to sleep for a couple of hours, you'll only feel worse. You might as well stay up."

"All night?" Molly said plaintively.

"Oh, don't be such a wimp. We have a murderer to catch. Who's at the top of the list?"

"Clark Dupree," Molly said resignedly. "Don't forget someone has to look into that Cayman bank account Patrice mentioned."

Liza wrote it down. "And I might as well put down Roger, Patrice, and myself since I know the police haven't given up on us yet."

"Don't forget Hernando Viera. He'd been having an affair with Tessa, too. And I guess we

167

can't leave off Jason Jeffries, though I'm certain he didn't do it."

Those notations made, Liza regarded her speculatively. "Who else?"

"It could have been anyone at the party."

"True, but realistically it must have been someone who knew Tessa well, unless some thief whacked her over the head just to take her jewels."

"Couldn't have been," Molly said. "She was still wearing that diamond ring that is worth a mint."

"So we're back to friends and acquaintances. How about the Willoughbys? And who's that other couple they're with all the time? He's a banker, too."

Molly recalled talking to them after the murder, though she hadn't known them before. "Newton?"

"No, Newcombe," Liza said.

"Right. Harley and Jane. He disliked everyone there," Molly recalled. "I'm not sure he disliked Tessa any more or less than anyone else."

"Maybe he plans to take them all out one by one."

"Liza!"

"Sorry. I'm getting punchy."

"What about Helen Whorton? She and Tessa had apparently been feuding for years. What's that rivalry all about?"

"I doubt they even recalled themselves. Tessa probably snatched all the glory after some event that Helen slaved over. In this crowd, that would certainly do it."

"Anyone else?"

Liza shook her head. "Not that I can think of. I'll go over the entire guest list later to see if anything rings a bell. Meantime, shouldn't we divide up these prospects and try to see what we can find out?"

"You know them," Molly reminded her. "I don't. Won't they think it downright peculiar if I come snooping around?"

"When was the last time that stopped you?"

"Okay, let's put it this way. If the opportunity presents itself, I will ask some questions."

Liza grinned in satisfaction. "Molly, dearest, haven't you learned that in life we make our own opportunities?"

Before Molly could respond to that barb, the phone rang. She glanced outside and saw that the sun was already sneaking over the horizon. "Michael, no doubt," she muttered as the phone continued to ring. "What on earth am I supposed to tell him?"

"The truth," Liza suggested.

Molly scowled at her as she grabbed the phone. "Good morning," she said with forced cheer.

"What happened?" Michael asked without preamble.

"I spoke with Hal last night," Molly said, hoping to divert him. "Thanks for the advice. I think it helped."

"I'm glad, but that's not what I'm talking about and you know it. Since Liza is not at home, I assume she is with you. I also deduce that you were together when she called Patrice MacDonald and have been plotting and scheming ever since."

"Why don't you come over and join us for breakfast?"

"Because I have exactly five minutes before I have to go and testify in a murder case. I would like to go with my mind at rest on other matters. Do you catch my drift here?"

"I do," Molly conceded. "We talked to her."

"And?"

"She's coming home today."

"Was that a decision she made before or after your call?" he inquired suspiciously.

"What does it matter? The point is she's coming home."

"You told her everything, didn't you?" he said, his tone somewhere between resigned and furious.

"I did not," Molly said flatly.

"Okay, Liza did. Don't play games. How

170

much does Mrs. MacDonald know about the current focus of this investigation?"

"Everything," Molly admitted reluctantly, then hurriedly added, "She says Clark Dupree did it."

He groaned. "Terrific. Does she have proof or do we have another amateur detective on our hands?"

"You don't have to be so cranky."

"Yes. I do," he said succinctly. "You two better spend today praying that our prime suspect shows her face."

"I would like to point out that you're the one who said we could call her," Molly retorted.

"I trusted you to use some discretion."

"We did the best we could."

"I'm sure," he muttered along with a few phrases of Spanish, which Molly felt sure were better left untranslated.

"He's furious," Liza guessed when Molly had hung up.

"I'd say that's an understatement. In fact, if you and I know what's good for us, we'll have this case solved before the end of the day or we'll be behind bars ourselves."

Liza looked startled. "He's that mad?"

"Mad enough to charge us with obstruction of justice, I'd say."

Liza ripped the yellow legal paper across the

middle and handed half to Molly. "Then let's get busy."

"Has it occurred to you that if we start running around questioning suspects, it will only add fuel to the fire?"

Liza shrugged. "Not if we catch the killer. That ought to take the wind right out of his sails."

CHAPTER
THIRTEEN

Since none of Molly's admittedly halfhearted protests had swayed Liza's newfound determination, it was fortunate that her boss at the film office chose to spend the day on the golf course again—doing business, according to him. Whatever, it left Molly free to indulge her best sleuthing techniques. Jeannette, however, scowled disapprovingly every time she started to make a phone call related to the case. Molly finally sent her to the location of a commercial shoot just so she wouldn't have to operate under her coworker's worried scrutiny.

Unfortunately, none of the calls she made turned up one single piece of evidence, much less a solid hint on motive. Hell, they didn't even turn up any of the suspects. Not even Ted Ryan, whom she'd planned to pump for information, was in his office. She decided against trying to track the reporter down at police headquarters, where Detective Abrams might get wind of her nosing around. He might take it well, but it wasn't his reaction she was worried about. Michael would blow sky-high.

Thoroughly frustrated, she opted finally for going to lunch. She would spend the hour trying to clear her head and consuming enough caffeine to keep her awake through the rest of the day. Tonight, if she had any energy left at all, she would kill Liza for getting her into this sorry state of exhaustion.

The players continued to taunt her as she drove from the Vizcaya gatehouse that contained the film office into the Grove. With Roger and Liza both more or less accounted for at the approximate time of Tessa's murder and Patrice MacDonald swearing she was innocent, Molly couldn't get Hernando Viera's affair with Tessa out of her mind. It had all the elements needed for a crime of passion.

What if Hernando had discovered that his mistress was already casting her eye about for another conquest? If Jason Jeffries was to be believed, the chase was far more important to Tessa than any lasting relationship, marital or illicit. That would explain her alleged affair with Clark Dupree.

Or, what if Caroline Viera knew all about her husband's fling and had tired of it? She might have challenged Tessa that night, argued heatedly with her, then cracked her over the skull with that silver candlestick. And then dragged her body all the way to the bay? Molly thought. Not likely. Still, she couldn't rule out anything.

By now the police must have retrieved the weapon from Neville's office. If Patrice hadn't taken it there, could Caroline Viera have been cool and composed enough to sneak it back into the caterer's domain? From what Molly had seen of her, yes. But her guesswork was no substitute for having a cozy little chat with the woman, who just happened to be sitting down for lunch—alone—across the crowded outdoor terrace of Tu Tu Tango, one of Cocowalk's liveliest restaurants in the heart of the Grove.

Molly squeezed between tables and gave Caroline one of her friendliest smiles. "How are you? Do you mind if I join you?"

Molly thought she caught a tiny flicker of fear in Caroline's eyes before she gestured resignedly.

"Of course not. I hate eating alone."

"So do I, especially in a place like this. Everyone always seems paired off. Do you come here often?"

"Whenever I have an appointment in this part of town. Several of my accounts are in Coconut Grove."

175

Caroline pushed her unopened menu aside as if to confirm that she knew every one of its appetizer-portion items by heart. Molly trumped the move with her own menu and a wave to get the attention of the waiter.

When their orders had been placed, Caroline surprised Molly by asking, "Have you heard anything about Tessa's murder?"

"Only that the list of suspects is no shorter than it was on the night it happened. What about you? Surely with Hernando's connections, he must have heard rumors." If the phrase *Hernando's connections* carried a double meaning for Caroline, she managed to hide her reaction. The woman was definitely a master of the polite mask.

"He hasn't mentioned anything to me," she said. "Of course, sometimes we're like two ships that pass in the night. We both have incredible business and social demands. Often we don't get home until midnight and Hernando is always out of the house at the crack of dawn."

Caroline's classic, angular face showed signs of the same weariness and resignation evident in her voice. Of course, guilt could be taxing, Molly thought just as Caroline added, "I don't know how Hernando does it."

"But I'm sure his dedication is one of the things that attracted you," Molly ventured, noting that Caroline seemed to diminish her own not inconsequential accomplishments and hectic schedule when comparing them to her husband's.

"That and the fact that he was terrific in bed," Caroline said with astonishing bluntness. It was the kind of remark deliberately meant to catch the listener off guard.

Dutifully startled, Molly met her gaze and saw that her lovely aquamarine eyes were filled with amusement.

"You're really no good at this," Caroline said. "If you want to know whether I know about Hernando's affair with Tessa, why don't you just ask me?"

Molly tried to hide her chagrin. "Obviously you do know," she said, then matched bluntness with candor. "Did you before the night of the murder?"

Caroline laughed, a full-bodied sound, rather than the nervous titter of someone guilty of a crime. "So you can be direct. Good. Perhaps we can be friends after all. Yes, I knew all about the affair before that night. I also knew about the dozen or more before Tessa and the half dozen waiting in the wings. I knew when I married Hernando fifteen years ago that he was no saint and that I wasn't going to be the one to change him. Our marriage, however, has its compensations."

"Which are?"

"I thought I'd mentioned the primary one."

"The sex. I suppose it comes from all that

practice," Molly said before she could stop herself.

"Indeed," Caroline agreed dryly. "Though these days I must admit I worry far more about the consequences of that than I did before."

"AIDS," Molly surmised.

"Yes."

"Still, I guess I can rule out your flying into a jealous rage that night and killing Tessa."

"Why on earth would I? Hernando had dismissed her and moved on. Frankly, if your friend Liza weren't so quick on her feet, I suspect she'd be next in line. She's gorgeous and intelligent. I believe Hernando describes her as a real hellion, something he definitely admires in a woman."

Molly decided it wasn't up to her to defend Liza's moral standards. She regarded Caroline with a certain amount of admiration. "Why am I beginning to suspect that a hellion is exactly what he got with you?"

Caroline nodded with evident satisfaction. "I may have to change my assessment, Molly. You might be quite good at this after all."

She glanced at the delicate, expensive gold watch on her wrist. The gesture also showed off an impressive diamond adorning a wide gold band on her ring finger. Either Caroline's business was extremely successful or Hernando paid for his transgressions with jewelry.

"My goodness, look at the time," she said. "I

178

have to run." She took a twenty out of her purse and put it on the table. "Lunch is on me this time. Let's do it again soon."

She picked up her Gucci briefcase and hurried off before Molly could protest her paying the bill or even say good-bye.

When she'd gone, Molly drew out the list she and Liza had compiled and scratched Caroline Viera's name off. Just as she did, a hand reached over her shoulder and plucked the paper off the table.

"What have we here?" Michael inquired, slipping into the chair just vacated by Caroline Viera. He'd dressed formally for his day in court. The dark pin-striped suit and pristine white shirt spoke more of Wall Street than it did Metro-Dade police headquarters. He looked drop-dead gorgeous, just as he had on the day they'd met.

Molly ignored the traitorous quickening of her pulse and regarded him warily. "What are you doing here?"

"Just hunting down suspects. How about you?"

"Am I a suspect now?"

"Nope, but who says I came here looking for you?"

Chagrined, Molly stared at him silently. He winked.

"Actually, I was told I'd find Caroline Viera here, but she was just taking off as I got to the front door. Then I caught a glimpse of you out here and figured you'd done all the advance work for me.''

"Oh?''

He glanced at the menu, ordered the pizza with sun-dried tomatoes, then regarded Molly with evident curiosity. "Is she guilty?''

"I don't appreciate your making fun of me,'' she said stiffly. "I'm trying to help.''

He held up his hands in a placating gesture. "I know that. And, actually, my question was a serious one. What's your take on Mrs. Viera?''

"Not guilty,'' she said succinctly and with complete conviction.

"No reasonable doubt?''

Molly's defensiveness fell away under his prodding. "I thought that applied to guilt, but no. I'm absolutely convinced she had no motive.''

"Not even her husband's affair with Tessa.''

"That's nothing out of the ordinary to hear her tell it.''

"She doesn't object to his affairs?''

"Apparently not.''

Michael looked doubtful. "Do you buy that understanding-woman crap?''

"Surprisingly enough, in this case, yes. And if she had finally gotten fed up, wouldn't she have killed Hernando rather than Tessa?''

"You have a point there. So who's next on this list of yours?'' he asked.

"Hernando."

"What about Clark Dupree? I thought he was Mrs. MacDonald's first choice."

"He's on Liza's list."

"Lord help me, now I've got two of you to keep tabs on?" he said with a moan. "Couldn't you work in tandem, so I can keep track of you?"

"We figured we didn't have much time. If the killer's not in custody by the end of the day, we had a hunch you'd drag us in for obstructing justice."

"The thought had crossed my mind," he admitted. "But I decided to leave that in the hands of the cop officially in charge of this case. Lucky for you, so far he hasn't heard about what the two of you did when you alerted Patrice MacDonald to the police interest in her whereabouts."

Molly breathed a sigh of relief. "Thank you."

"Don't thank me yet. Just pray his suspect turns up."

"Or that we come up with a better one," Molly countered.

"That would do," he agreed.

Molly regarded him curiously. "Are you officially on or off this case?"

"Officially, off. But Abrams has said he'd be more than glad of all the unofficial help I can offer."

"Which makes your status only slightly better

than mine," Molly said with satisfaction. "Want to go with me to see Hernando?"

"What's your excuse for dropping in?"

"I thought I'd make a donation to Tessa's memorial fund. He's in charge."

Michael nodded, then took a last sip of his iced tea. "Let's go."

They found Hernando Viero in his spartan office atop the downtown skyscraper where his bank was headquartered. The only thing lavish was the view of Biscayne Bay and the whitecapped waves of the Atlantic before them. On the bay at full mast was a tall ship, which took tourists out of Bayside on a tour along the Brickell Avenue skyline, under the Rickenbacker Causeway and past Vizcaya, the scene of the crime.

"Thank you for seeing us without an appointment," Molly said to the bank president, who'd obviously taken the downfall of another banker down the street to heart. The most expensive thing in the office was Hernando's custom-tailored suit in a shade of gunmetal gray that matched the distinguished traces in his hair and mustache. Everything else in the office was tasteful, but barely more than functional. If he had any art objects or gold fixtures around, they were well hidden.

"It's always a pleasure," he said. "What can I do for the two of you?"

"We wanted to see how Tessa's memorial

fund is coming. I have a contribution right here," Molly said, taking a check from her purse. She'd drawn it on the trust fund set up by her parents years ago, money she'd sworn she'd never touch except in a dire emergency. In this instance, the cause seemed worthy of breaking that vow. She supposed there was a certain bitter irony in the fact that she knew they'd object to the cause.

"Wonderful," Hernando said, putting the check in a stack on his desk without glancing at the amount. "Actually, the fund is doing quite well. I think Roger and Liza will be pleased. Has Liza given any thought to how the funds would be disbursed?"

Molly shook her head. "I don't believe so, but she is planning an emergency meeting of the coalition board this week. I'm sure that will be on the agenda." She glanced at Michael as she prepared to shift gears in the way they'd discussed on the drive downtown. "Hernando, have you noticed anything unusual about the contributions made thus far?"

His gaze narrowed thoughtfully. "Unusual in what way?"

"Perhaps from someone unexpected? Perhaps in an amount larger than expected?"

"No, but then I haven't been looking for anything like that. I've just been grateful for every dollar that came in for Tessa's sake."

"Could we see the list of donors?"

"I don't see why not. It'll certainly be a matter of public record once it's turned over to the coalition anyway. Nonprofits are very careful about their record keeping." He pulled a folder from his desk drawer and handed it to Molly. She passed it straight on to Michael.

As he studied the pages in the folder, Molly tried to find an inoffensive way to phrase her next question. There wasn't one. "Hernando, your relationship with Tessa . . ."

He sighed wearily. "Puts me on the list of suspects. I know that. It was over for Tessa and me. Quite some time ago, as a matter of fact. I believe she considered me a daring indulgence."

Molly was startled by the odd description. "Why on earth would she feel that way?"

"Surely, you know that those in Tessa's circle have yet to fully adapt to the new Miami. Many of them resent the Cubans, whom they feel have taken over. I am tolerated in those circles, because I have a certain power, but I am not liked. If Tessa had chosen to have an affair with a declared criminal, it would have been no less risky for her."

To Molly's astonishment there was little bitterness in his voice, just resignation, perhaps even a measure of understanding for those Anglos who'd been unable to adapt readily to the new Miami power structure in which they were no longer in the majority.

184

"But despite everything, you and Roger seemed almost cordial the other day," she said. "If what you say is true, wouldn't he be outraged by the affair?"

"Perhaps things are not as they seem," he suggested enigmatically.

Michael glanced up at that, indicating that he had not been quite as absorbed in the paperwork as he'd led them to believe. "In what way?"

"Roger Lafferty owes a great deal of money to this bank. That is yet another reason for him to resent me. However, it is also an excellent reason to remain on friendly terms. Despite his business reversals, Roger is no fool. However he feels about me personally, he will not allow those feelings to show in public. In fact, he has found himself of necessity being my champion among his friends."

"Could all that resentment have boiled over the night of the gala?"

"You mean could he have taken it out on Tessa, since he didn't dare take it out on me? Possible, but doubtful. You see, for all of his indignation over her behavior, Roger still loved Tessa."

"There's a rumor that he planned to divorce her," Molly said.

Hernando appeared genuinely startled by that. "I doubt it. I don't think he would ever have willingly let her go."

"And if she pressed for a divorce, insisted on it?" Michael asked.

Hernando looked troubled as he contemplated that. "Then, yes," he said very softly, regretfully. "Under such a circumstance, he might very well have killed her, rather than let her go."

CHAPTER
FOURTEEN

There were far too many unanswered questions about Roger Lafferty, in Molly's opinion. In Michael's, too, for that matter. She could see it in his eyes when Hernando admitted that Roger was capable of killing Tessa to keep from losing her.

However, when she broached the possibility of paying another visit to the bereaved widower, Michael balked, digging in his heels with all the machismo he was capable of mustering.

"No way. Absolutely not. Forget it." He peered at her intently. "Have I made myself clear?"

She flinched under that steady gaze, though she was somewhat less intimidated than she would have been a few months earlier. "Perfectly. So, what do we do next?"

"Nothing. You go back to work. I go back to work. And we let Detective Abrams do his job."

"That is getting to be a very old refrain," Molly pointed out.

"But a prudent one," he said, dropping a light kiss on her forehead. This time it didn't have the dizzying effect he'd probably hoped for. Molly was still thinking clearly and resentfully.

"Go back to work," he repeated. He pointed in the general direction of South Miami Avenue to make sure she got the message.

"Back to work," she repeated prudently. "Right."

By the time she reached her car in the bank's parking garage, she'd already figured out whom she could speak to about Roger without violating Michael's direct order. It was certainly convenient, too, that Clark Dupree's luxurious suite of legal offices was on Brickell, right on her way back to the film office.

Molly noted right off that representing bigtime developers obviously paid a bundle. Clark's teal carpet was every bit as thick as Jason Jeffries's down the block. The art in the reception area was by Jackson Pollock and other lesser-known, but no less pricey, contemporary American masters. Maybe it was just an aura created by the classic, subdued gallery lighting, but Molly was certain the paintings were the real thing.

"May I help you?"

The voice was low, cultured, and classy enough to do voice-overs on British television productions. Molly decided the accent was a nice touch. She could see how it would appeal to Clark's desire to create a refined image. It probably made the sleazy characters he represented feel cultured as well. Too bad it was deceptive.

"I'd like to see Mr. Dupree," Molly told the woman whose thick waves of honey-colored hair skimmed shoulders clad in tasteful silk. "I'm Molly DeWitt."

"Do you have an appointment?"

She gave a cursory glance at the mammoth, leather-bound appointment book, but she knew as well as Molly did what she'd find there. Or what she wouldn't. She probably memorized his calendar by eight each morning.

"No, actually I was hoping to catch him between appointments." Molly offered an apologetic smile. "I know how busy he must be, but if you could fit me in for just a few minutes, I swear I won't take up much of his time."

"Is this an emergency of some sort?"

"Life or death," Molly said without batting an eye.

The woman's gaze turned unexpectedly kind and gentle. "I'll do the best I can."

Every boss should have a receptionist like this one, Molly thought. She was better than Muzak at soothing anxious visitors. While she prepared to wait, Molly took a seat on a chair upholstered in an elegant fabric that reminded her of something she'd seen in Vizcaya. If Clark outfitted his office like this, what on earth must his home be like? she wondered.

She tried to listen as the receptionist spoke to someone deep in the suite's interior, but that cultured voice had dropped to a discreet murmur. Occasional glances in Molly's direction suggested she was the primary topic of conversation.

Finally the receptionist turned to Molly with a pleased expression. "Mrs. Murchison will see you now."

Molly regarded her blankly. "Who is she?"

"Mr. Dupree's executive assistant. I'm sure she'll be able to help you."

The only help Molly needed was getting past this efficient, feminine security system. She took a chance that Mrs. Murchison would be less stalwart than the receptionist. She had her doubts. She had a hunch the security got tighter the closer one got to the inner sanctum.

Sure enough, Mrs. Murchison looked her over as if checking for weapons. "I'm afraid Mr. Dupree's calendar doesn't permit unscheduled appointments," she said, after deciding that Molly was neither dangerous, nor in grave danger of dropping dead on the spot. Other emergencies probably didn't count for much around here.

"Five minutes," Molly said, trying not to beg. "I swear I won't take any longer than that."

"I'm sorry, but Mr. Dupree is out of the office at the moment anyway."

Molly regarded her doubtfully. Why would either one of these women have gone through with this charade if that were true? The first wave of the guard would have sent her packing. Unfortunately, she couldn't see any way to call her on it short of declaring her a liar or plopping into a chair and waiting to see if Clark eventually came into or out of his office. It hardly seemed worth the energy, especially when she had no concrete plan for effectively cross-examining him once she got inside.

She removed one of her business cards from her purse and handed it to Mrs. Murchison. As she did, she glanced at the bank of phone lines. Several were lit. Two were blinking, but another two were clearly engaged. There were no other legal partners, to Molly's knowledge, not even space for a law clerk. Therefore, unless the receptionist had the ability to speak with more than one person at a time, Clark Dupree himself was on that other line. She gestured toward the phone.

"Give him the card when he gets off the phone and ask him to call me when he gets a chance," she said, leaving the woman staring after her in openmouthed astonishment.

Disgruntled by her lack of success and curious about Clark Dupree's apparent reticence to see her, she was halfway back to the office, when she remembered Josie, the Laffertys' dedicated housekeeper. Josie clearly had tales to tell. Molly wondered if she'd care to tell them to her.

She made a quick right turn off of Brickell and headed over to Coral Way, then drove on through the Gables to the Lafferty house. Though there were no cars in the driveway this time, she intended to take no chances on encountering Roger. If she could get past the guard without being questioned, she'd go around to the side door and look for Josie in the kitchen.

The guard, the same one who'd been on duty on her last visit, waved—either in recognition or as a signal of general apathy, then went back to the magazine he'd been reading. Apparently it was absorbing enough or he was so unobservant that he didn't notice her odd route straight past the front door and around to the side of the house.

If Josie was surprised to see her at the kitchen door, she hid it well. Maybe she'd just been around so long that nothing much struck her as peculiar. She waved Molly into the kitchen.

"I've been baking a bit," she announced unnecessarily. The huge room with its restaurant-sized stove and ovens was fragrant with the sweet aroma of fruit pies and the nutty, cinnamon scent of coffee cakes. The results of her labors were lined up along one tiled counter. If she did many more, she'd have to open a bakery to get rid of them all.

"Can't seem to keep my mind on anything else," she explained with a shrug. "I figure we'll be needing these before things are done. If not, they freeze up right well. You want to try a piece of my strawberry pie? Ain't nothing like it in any of those fancy restaurants around town." She chuckled. "I know that 'cause I've had a couple of big-time caterers beg me to turn over that recipe."

"Neville Foster was one of them, I'll bet," Molly said as she took the first mouth-watering bite of the sweet concoction with a crust so flaky it melted. "Josie, you deserve a place of honor in heaven for your baking. Neville's customers have probably had this pie here and dreamed of serving it in their own homes."

"Wouldn't give it to the likes of him," she said with an indignant huff.

There was so much derision in her tone that Molly regarded her in astonishment. "You don't like him?"

"He's a sneaky little so-and-so. Wouldn't put it past him to snoop through my cupboards trying to steal my recipes. Caught him at it once, in fact. He claimed he was looking for the rest of the champagne glasses, but he couldn't fool me."

She winked at Molly. "Lot of good it did him. I got my recipes hidden where no one can get at 'em." She tapped her head. "Every one of 'em is right up here."

Molly nearly moaned at the thought of losing all those old-fashioned recipes if Josie didn't pass them on before she died. Obviously, for the moment though, the tough old bird had no intention of dying or giving away her secrets. Molly ate the last crumb of her pie and drank some of the herbal iced tea Josie had poured for her. The housekeeper was regarding her speculatively.

"I suppose you got a reason for dropping by to see old Josie?"

Molly considered trying to finesse her way around the old woman's sharp intuition, but opted for being straightforward instead.

"I'm trying to figure some things out," she said candidly. "I've got all these questions going around in my head. I thought maybe you could help me fill in some of the blanks."

"About Miz Tessa?" Josie said, losing some of her vim and vigor. She suddenly looked her age.

"That's right."

"It surely doesn't make a bit of sense to me either," she said, sitting down heavily. "Why would someone go killing a lady like her?"

"You said yourself that she had her flaws."

"She did that, but not the sort of things to go getting killed over," she declared indignantly.

"She made Mr. Roger madder than a wet hen sometimes, but I never heard him say a mean word to her."

"They didn't argue?"

"No more than most married folks."

"I'd heard he was thinking of divorcing her."

Josie looked convincingly shocked. "Never! Not Mr. Roger. He didn't believe in divorce."

"I thought she'd been divorced before."

"That was all in the past. Had nothing to do with the two of them. Besides, he adored that woman, no matter what. He turned a blind eye to her faults. Now if her own husband could put up with all her craziness, who else would have reason to hurt her?"

"By all her craziness, I assume you mean the other men," Molly said carefully.

Josie hesitated, clearly uncertain over whether an admission could be considered disloyal. Apparently she decided it was too late to worry about such things. She nodded. "It puzzles me why a high-class woman would behave like that. It just wasn't right and I told her so more than once. She had everything she could ever need or want. Mr. Roger saw to that. She said to me herself that he was a saint." Josie shook her head sorrowfully. "Didn't make no difference. There was always some other man waiting in the wings."

"Any particular man lately?"

"She never told me their names 'cause she

knew I disapproved. I could just tell when there was a new one on the horizon.'' She regarded Molly confidingly. "You know what the problem was? Low self-esteem. I saw that on Oprah or Geraldo, one of them shows. It was all about women who need a new man all the time to prove how desirable they are. If I'd been able to figure out that fancy VCR machine in the other room, I'd have put that on tape and made Miz Tessa watch it a time or two till she saw things right again.'' She shook her head. "Low self-esteem. Who would have thought it?''

The concept clearly bemused her almost as much as it distressed her that Tessa might have been a victim of the syndrome.

"But why would Tessa have low self-esteem?'' Molly asked, trying to reconcile that with the image of arrogance she presented to the world.

"Now that's a question you'd have to be asking one of them fancy head doctors.''

"Are you sure about that? Low self-esteem usually begins in childhood. You said you were hired by her family when she was still a girl. What were her parents like?''

"They were fine people,'' Josie insisted. "Helped me educate my brothers and sisters. Got 'em all through high school. Two of my brothers even went on to college, thanks to her daddy's help. Same college Miz Tessa's brother went to.''

"What about Tessa? Did she go to college?"

Josie looked perplexed by the question. "Now, why would she need to do that? She had her path in life all cut out for her. She had plenty of money to see that she made the right kind of marriage. Wasn't no need for her to get some fancy education that would just be wasted."

"Is that what her father said?" Molly asked, beginning to get the picture.

"Told her that time and again," Josie confirmed.

"So she wanted to go to college?"

"Had some crazy fool notion about becoming a business tycoon. She wanted to run her daddy's company someday, but everybody knew her brother was going to do that, so what was the point? If you ask me, she should have been satisfied with the way things were."

Maybe so, Molly thought as she drove off a short time later. Maybe Tessa should have played by the rules of the day and been satisfied, but obviously that niche envisioned by her short-sighted father hadn't been enough for her. No wonder she'd constantly sought the approval of powerful, successful men. She'd wanted to prove she could hold her own with any one of them.

For the first time since the investigation had begun, Molly began to feel desperately sorry for the pathetic life Tessa had led in her ill-fated quest for proof that she was somebody important. She couldn't help wondering if that same quest wasn't in some obscure way responsible for her murder.

CHAPTER
FIFTEEN

Molly was so intent on learning all she could about Tessa's need for approval and yearning for business success, she didn't notice at first that Vince had finally wandered back to the office.

"Where have you been?" her boss demanded, glancing pointedly at the oversized clock on the wall. The look was mostly for effect. The clock hadn't been right for months now.

"You're in a charming mood," she observed. "What happened? Did you double bogey on the eighteenth hole?"

"The game isn't everything," he shot back, scowling ferociously. "I conduct business on the golf course. I was trying to close a deal out there."

"Oh?"

"I might have done it if I'd been able to reach anyone in this office for some information. Instead, all I got was a recording. Why the hell should I have a staff, if no one's ever here?"

Molly took the attack in stride. Naturally, now that Vince was off the golf course, he wanted everyone to be as miserable and put-upon as he was. It was Vincent Gates's nature to present a long-suffering facade to the world. He thought it would keep his job secure if his superiors thought he was dreadfully overburdened with work.

"What information did you need?" she inquired sweetly. "I'll be happy to get it and follow up with a phone call to the producer."

"Never mind," he grumbled, clearly happy sulking. "I've taken care of it. Where's Jeannette?" He gave a furtive glance around as if to assure himself she wasn't lurking in the vicinity ready to cast some evil spell over him.

"On location. When are you going to admit that she's the best clerk we've ever had in here and put in for a promotion for her?"

"Don't start on me again."

"You're hoping she'll just give up and go away, aren't you? I've told her she ought to do just that. She's overqualified for this job. Any other boss would appreciate her."

"I do appreciate her. She just makes me nervous. You've seen the way she looks at me."

Molly bit back a grin. Jeannette's cool, superior looks embodied disdain, not malevolence, but Vince would never believe that. It was probably best not to explain either. He was already regarding her suspiciously.

"I suppose you were on location, too?"

"Nope. I had some personal business to take care of."

Vince didn't have to ponder that more than a heartbeat before he caught on. He rolled his eyes in exasperation. "Not again. Tell me you were not out snooping around on that murder investigation."

She remained stoically silent.

He watched her intently. "You were, weren't you? That's exactly what you were doing. When will you ever learn?" He held up his hands in a gesture of resignation. "I give up. The next time I get called on the carpet by some county official because you can't stay out of things that are none of your concern, you are out of here. Adios. Good-bye. Is that clear?"

Molly nodded obediently, which usually made Vince feel powerful again. "Must have been a triple bogey," she muttered under her breath as she returned to her desk.

"I heard that," he shouted after her.

Hopefully he wouldn't hear her conversation with Jason Jeffries, she thought as she dialed the philanthropist's office. She had to check out this one last thing while it was on her mind. Then she vowed to get busy and actually do some film office business. It would pacify Vince if he ended the day with a stack of folders on prospective productions sitting on his desk. He could complain to his date all evening about how backed up he was at work.

"What sort of information are you after this time, young lady?" the old man said, an affectionate note behind the cranky question.

"I want to talk about Tessa a minute."

"What about her?"

"Josie . . ."

"Her housekeeper? I didn't even know she was still alive. She must be a hundred, if she's a day."

"She says she's seventy. She also told me that Tessa had some crazy notion of becoming a business tycoon and that her father thwarted her because he didn't see any need to educate a woman."

"Never heard it told quite that way, but I suppose it's true enough," he conceded. "Tessa envied that brother of hers. She resented the fact that he was destined to inherit the business, while all she got was some trust fund. She'd been daddy's little darling all her life until the time came to divvy up the estate. Then he put her in her place. Wasn't all that unusual given the way things worked in those days."

"Could she have run the business?"

Jason gave a snort of derision. "I told you about the books on those fund-raisers. Does that sound like the kind of woman who could manage a big corporation? Tessa had grandiose ideas, but not an ounce of sense when it came to carrying them out. If you ask me, her daddy knew exactly what he was doing. Hell, I doled out her alimony payments a little at a time, because I knew damned well she'd throw it all away and come begging for more if I didn't."

"Thanks," Molly said, unwilling to get into a debate over whether Tessa might have learned to handle money if she'd been given a little responsibility and education. It was too late for such a discussion to do the woman a bit of good, and she doubted if Jason was likely to change his sexist ways at this late date either.

Unless Liza could turn him around. The thought of the struggle brought a smile to her lips.

"I don't know why any of that's important, but you're welcome," he said. His tone sobered. "You watch where you go sniffing around, young lady. Whoever killed Tessa might see a need to get rid of you, too, if you start getting too close to the truth."

Coming from any of the other principal suspects, Molly might have considered that a mild threat. Coming from Jason Jeffries, it seemed no more than a friendly, concerned warning. She took it to heart.

That didn't stop her from trying to add things up one more time. What if Tessa, in her zeal to prove that she was capable of handling business as well as any man, had gotten herself in over her head? They'd assumed all along that Roger was responsible for whatever financial difficulties he was having, but what if it had been Tessa's foolish decisions that had been their downfall?

Perhaps that had been the one thing Roger couldn't forgive, despite Josie's faith that he would tolerate any of Tessa's myriad sins. Not all that long ago there had been stories in Japan about wives who'd lost the family savings in the stock market and were so terrified of their husbands' wrath that they committed suicide or begged their brokers to hide the truth. Maybe Tessa had suffered a similar humiliation and had infuriated Roger in the process.

Molly decided she needed to see all the suspects together if she was ever going to fully understand the dynamics of the group. For that, she needed Liza's help. If Vince's menacing scowl was anything to go by, however, she figured she'd better wait to ask her.

● ● ●

"Liza, why don't you organize that emergency coalition meeting you've been talking about?"

Molly suggested later that night after concluding a reasonably productive afternoon at the office under Vince's watchful eye. "I suppose we could wait for the memorial service, but I heard it's been delayed until late next week. I don't want to put this off that long. I think it would be fascinating to see what the primary topic of conversation is about now, don't you?"

Liza regarded her doubtfully. "You don't honestly expect the killer to confess sometime between the reading of the minutes and old business, do you?"

"I'm not even sure I expect him or her to show up."

"Meaning?"

"We're not dealing with a professional killer here. Whoever murdered Tessa probably did it on the spur of the moment. Unless he or she has absolutely no conscience, the person who tossed Tessa into the bay might find it incredibly awkward to be surrounded by all of her dearest friends."

"Friends?"

"You know what I mean. Who's on the coalition board?"

"Patrice, Mary Ann Willoughby, Helen Whorton, Jason Jeffries, Hernando Viera, and Clark Dupree are on the executive board. The overall committee is much larger. Which group do you want?"

205

"I'd say the executive board covers the key people. Can you meet in closed session?"

"Not really. We take the Sunshine Law to heart. All our meetings are open."

"I suppose it doesn't really matter. What about Roger? Can you lure him there?"

Liza considered the question, her expression thoughtful. "I suppose I could ask him so we can make the official announcement of Tessa's memorial fund."

Molly nodded. "Perfect."

Liza shook her head. "Why do I think that instead of inviting them to a meeting, I should simply announce 'let the games begin'?"

"An interesting alternative," Molly concurred. "But this is no game. Whoever killed Tessa obviously had a lot more than we know at stake and I want to know what that was."

CHAPTER
SIXTEEN

Molly wouldn't have believed the viciousness if she hadn't been seeing it with her own eyes. A half dozen of the best-known names in Miami's philanthropic circles—male and female—were engaged in cutthroat politics that made Republican and Democratic rivalries look like kid stuff.

Observers from several organizations had learned of the meeting of the coalition's executive board and had shown up to stick in their two cents. Michael O'Hara and Detective Abrams, after casting pleased looks at their suspect, just back from London, were lurking in the back of the room, trying to look unobtrusive. They weren't succeeding, but their presence definitely wasn't hampering the discussion or Patrice MacDonald's glares in their direction.

In the absence of a chairman, Liza explained that she had called the group together to discuss the future of the consortium of environmental activists. Their common interests should have assured a certain unanimity.

Instead, the supporters of the Everglades were casting venomous glances at the bird people, who in turn were scowling at those in support of the manatees. The representatives of one of the nation's most active environmental preservation organizations were regarding Florida Keys protectionists with visible disdain.

Helen Whorton, Tessa's most outspoken rival, was surveying the scene with satisfaction. From the sidelines where Molly had determinedly planted herself despite Liza's request that she sit around the conference table, Molly guessed Helen was just waiting for the right opportunity to leap graciously into the leadership breach. She was shooting daggers at Liza because she hadn't gotten out of the way.

Jason Jeffries, clearly an independent thinker and a member of every organization represented, winked at Liza. "Go get 'em," he said in what was no doubt meant to be an undertone but which boomed to the back of the room. Startled glances turned in his direction.

"Ladies and gentlemen," Liza said so softly that those present had to quiet down or risk missing something they might find irritating. "If we continue to focus on our divided loyalties, rather than the unified mission we need so desperately to complete, we will have no chance at all."

"Well said," Jeffries commented, waving his cigar approvingly. It was unlit in deference to Molly. "I'll nominate you to chair this group. Who'll second it?"

"Now wait just one minute, Jason Jeffries!" Helen Whorton glared at him. "You won't go ramroding your opinion down our throats this time."

"That's right," Mary Ann Willoughby chimed in, then looked startled that she'd found herself on the same side as Tessa's most vociferous enemy.

"There is a motion on the floor," Liza said firmly. "It requires a second before we can have this discussion."

"I'll second," said a timid voice belonging to a woman who looked as if she ought to be traipsing the trails of the Everglades with a pair of binoculars in her hands. To get Liza's attention, she allowed her fingers to flutter in the air for no more than an instant before demurely folding her hands in her lap again.

"Thank you," Liza said, giving her an appreciative smile. "Now, Helen, what were you saying?"

"I was saying that I will not allow that man to push this through."

"Oh, for goodness' sake, Helen, sit down and shut up," said a tall string bean of a man who was gray from head to toe—hair, suit, socks, shoes, even his complexion had an unhealthy gray pallor. Since he'd said the first sensible thing in the past few minutes, Molly hoped he didn't pass out before they could take a vote.

"You know perfectly well that Liza is the only one here who's actually put her money and her time into this," he declared with annoyance. "She's been to the rain forests. She's protested the haphazard forestry in Washington and Oregon. She's been to Capitol Hill to speak out. She's prepared position papers and lobbied Congress. What the dickens have you ever done besides yammer about it?"

Helen's eyes widened with shock. "How dare you, Lincoln Granview? My name alone counts for plenty and I have given generous donations to these causes besides."

"When it suited your purposes," he countered. "You want the social power. I saw you scrambling to get in one of those pictures for the society pages in the morning paper. Plunked yourself right in there next to Tessa, even though everyone knows you hated her guts. You want to appear politically correct. But you obviously don't give a damn about the environment or you wouldn't have allowed your husband to strip that land in the Keys bare before he built on it."

An outraged murmur built in the room until Molly had visions of a lynch mob being formed. Given the passion with which these people regarded their individual causes, it didn't require a giant leap of faith to accept the possibility that one of them might have murdered Tessa if they felt she'd betrayed them. Molly could hardly wait to question Liza about how each of the attendees had interacted with the recently departed chairwoman, about how much faith they'd had in her dedication to the cause.

"That's enough," Liza said, quieting things down again. "The floor is open to additional nominations." She glanced pointedly at her most vocal critic. "Helen?"

"I suppose there's no point in my going against the majority." She scowled first at Liza, then at Lincoln Granview, finally settling her gaze on Jason Jeffries. "You will get yours one of these days. If not here on earth, then I'm certain there's a special hell waiting for you."

That said, she pulled herself to her feet and stalked from the room.

"Good riddance," Jeffries muttered. "Now let's get on with business. Call for a vote, Liza."

Liza frowned at him. "Jason, if you don't stop giving me orders, people here might begin to wonder if Helen wasn't right to object to my nomination."

He beamed back at her approvingly. "Well said. You'll do just fine, girl."

Just then Ted Ryan slipped into the room and made his way straight to Molly's side. Michael shot her a wry look as he observed the maneuver.

"What did I miss?" the journalist asked, pulling out his pocket tape recorder and a notebook.

"Liza has been nominated to chair the group. They're about to vote."

"Where's the old battle-ax?" he inquired, glancing around.

Molly regarded him with feigned innocence. "Who?"

"Old lady Whorton."

"I believe she had another pressing engagement," Molly said, deciding that the less said in the media about today's squabble, the better for all concerned. If Helen wanted to make a fool of herself in print, let her call Ted herself and fill him in.

With Liza's election approved by the majority in a vote taken by secret ballot at Mary Ann's insistence, Molly sat back and waited for the routine business of the group to be concluded.

Several mundane reports were given regarding the status of various projects. To her disappointment, none struck Molly as being particularly controversial.

Liza called for new business. When no one spoke out, she said, "We do have two things I'd like to mention. First, I would like to formally express the board's condolences to Roger Lafferty."

Sympathetic glances were cast in his direction. He acknowledged them with a nod.

"As many of you know, Roger graciously determined to open a memorial fund in Tessa's honor. Hernando, I understand we have a first check for the coalition from that fund," Liza said.

The banker stood and gave a courtly half bow in Liza's direction. If his gaze lingered appreciatively an instant longer than necessary, Molly figured she was the only one who noticed. Caroline had planted the idea of Hernando's interest in Liza in her head. Liza seemed oblivious.

"We owe Roger a great debt of gratitude for allowing us to establish this memorial fund in honor of his wife," Hernando said. "Today it is my pleasure to present the coalition with a check in the amount of two hundred and fifty thousand dollars, which accounts for the contributions to date. I have no doubt that with the proper administration this fund will continue to grow."

Molly gasped at the amount that had accumulated in such a short time. She wondered if a single guilty donor had been responsible for pushing the fund well into six figures. As she wondered about that, Roger stood up.

His normally strong voice shook with emotion as he said, "I would like to thank many of you in this room for your generosity. Tessa believed deeply that we have a responsibility to preserve what nature has given us. I hope that this fund will provide support to many environmental causes and that it will make the sort of difference she would have made had she lived to see things through."

"Hear, hear!" Jason Jeffries said, showing considerably more enthusiasm for his ex-wife in death than he had in life. "I think we should form a special task force to determine how these funds should be allocated."

Liza glanced at Roger. "Perhaps you would like to chair such a task force."

He regarded her uncertainly. "I'm not sure that I would be the best person . . ." His voice trailed off.

"Enough of that. Of course you would," Patrice said firmly, ready to rally the troops around him now that his wife was gone. "I am willing to serve as well. Lincoln?"

"Of course."

Liza smiled. "Then I think we have our committee." She paused to lead the group in a round of applause for the new task force. Molly observed the others in the room closely. All seemed to be joining in wholeheartedly. It was the first time all day they'd been unified about anything.

"Now there is one more piece of business," Liza said, her tone suddenly more grave. "Something has come to my attention just today that I think we ought to take a stand on. Yet another proposal is before the Dade County Commission regarding development in the western part of the county.''

''The wetlands?'' asked one horrified listener. ''Surely not again.''

''Yes, again, I'm sorry to say. There have been some changes on the federal level and local developers have taken that as a sign to try one more time to push progress straight into the Everglades.''

An outraged murmur spread around the room. ''Who's at it this time?'' Patrice demanded. She glared at Clark, then looked pointedly at Michael as if willing him to share her suspicions. ''I'm sure you could tell us that,'' she told Clark. ''You're probably representing the devils.''

''No, I am not,'' he said, returning her scowl without flinching.

From the sparks flying between the two, Molly figured it was safe to assume that the pair had removed the kid gloves and intended an all-out battle of wills.

''Stop pussyfooting around, Clark,'' Patrice demanded. ''You know perfectly well that if there's a dollar to be made on development in this town, you know the players.''

''I do stay on top of things, yes,'' he said agreeably. ''That's not a crime, Patrice. It's a civic responsibility. You should do the same.''

"I'd say 'on top' is the wrong phrase. 'In the middle' would be more like it." She sat back with a satisfied smirk.

Liza apparently decided that the squabble wasn't gaining the group a single bit of information and might well deteriorate into something truly ugly.

"Enough, you two," she said quietly. "I just learned about this today and didn't have time to research it myself. The person who called me right before the meeting did mention the name of the company, Danson Properties, Inc. Has anyone ever heard of it?"

No one acknowledged being familiar with the company. Molly kept her gaze pinned on Clark Dupree, but his expression remained stoic. She couldn't help wondering if the look expressed genuine bafflement or had been perfected to keep from revealing too much. It certainly would be handy in a courtroom. Either way it was clear that details would not be forthcoming from him.

"Would anyone like to propose a statement for the media regarding our stance on this?" Liza suggested.

"Perhaps we should consider getting more information before we go off half-cocked," Clark Dupree suggested mildly. He avoided Patrice's gaze when he said it.

"Of course you'd want us to remain silent,"

she snapped. "The less said by the opposition, the better to get county approval."

"No," Liza said reasonably. "What Clark suggests makes sense. We don't want to get a reputation for crying wolf, unless the proposed development is truly a threat to the Everglades. Why don't I look into it and then we can schedule another meeting for next week to firm up our position?"

"What if the commission decides to ramrod it through before that?" Lincoln Granview demanded.

"Any resolution would require more than one reading before the commission," Liza reminded him. "We're not even sure if this has zoning or planning approval. I'll check it out as soon as we leave here today. If I find out it's further along in the process than that, I will notify each of you and we can make plans to appear before the commission to outline our objections. In the meantime, if you require inspiration to remind you of what the fight is all about, reread *River of Grass*. Marjorie Stoneman Douglas said it all in her classic book on the Everglades."

"Perhaps we should send copies to the commissioners," Jason suggested dryly.

Patrice regarded him approvingly. "Good idea, Jason. I'll do that myself."

With that the meeting adjourned. To Molly's disappointment, the killer had not revealed himself or herself. That had been too much to hope for, she supposed.

When Liza was finally able to join her, she said, "When exactly did you hear about this development deal? You didn't mention it on the way over here."

"I got a call here right before the meeting started. It was all very mysterious. The caller wouldn't even identify himself."

"Did you recognize anything about the voice?" Michael inquired as he joined them.

Liza shook her head. "I was too furious about the message to worry about the messenger. I wish it hadn't been so last-minute. If I'd had time to check it out, we could have taken a formal stand today and Ted Ryan could have gotten it in tomorrow's paper. I want these people on notice that they won't be able to sneak this through."

She glanced at Molly, her expression genuinely distraught. "Every time I think about these random attacks on the fragile ecology of the Everglades, it makes me sick. There's nothing else like it in the United States. We should be protecting it, not destroying it just to put up another strip mall or plunk down another community of tacky, matching houses."

It was a subject on which Molly shared Liza's views and her fervor. "Half the malls we have now are failing because there are too many of them," she chimed in. "The last time I drove into one of these new developments, most of the houses were unoccupied, the developer had run out of funds, and there was a suit from the few existing home-owners to force him to make good on the ameni-ties he'd promised. They'd read about a similar mess in California that made a deal with the pro-ducers of *Lethal Weapon* to wipe the whole thing out. The homeowners invited me out because they wondered if we had any films coming into town that might want to destroy their community as part of the plot."

"So why would anyone want to build another one?" Michael asked.

Molly sensed that the question was rhetorical, but Liza jumped right in to answer anyway.

"I'll tell you why," she said furiously. "Greed. Pure and simple."

"Greed," Molly echoed thoughtfully. "Re-member when we said the key to solving Tessa's murder was to find the money. Maybe this is it."

Liza looked startled by the suggestion, but then she nodded. "You could be right. How do we find out the principals in this deal?"

"I'll make a few calls to a friend in another county department, and if the lid on this isn't on too tight, we should know in no time." Molly glanced at Michael to get his reaction to the plan.

He shrugged. "It wouldn't hurt to make the call. If you unearth something, though, call me or

Detective Abrams. Don't go chasing down any leads yourselves."

After promising to be careful, Liza broke speed limits getting them back to Molly's office so she could make the call. Unfortunately, the only official record of the zoning request listed no more than the name of the company, Danson Properties, Inc.

Discouraged, Molly hung up the phone. "No luck."

Liza, however, was just getting her second wind. "Don't look so glum. If it's incorporated, then there are records on file with the state. I'll call Tallahassee."

"Do you have a contact who'll do the digging for you?"

Liza grinned. "I have contacts everywhere they might come in handy. You should know that by now."

It took one call and a half hour of impatient pacing to get the answer they were after. When the call came in, Molly reluctantly handed the phone over to Liza, then had to watch as a slow grin spread across her face, only to twist into something else entirely. There were furious sparks in her eyes by the time she hung up.

"Well?" Molly demanded.

"The president of Danson Properties, Inc. is none other than our good friend and board member Clark Dupree."

Molly started to speak, but Liza held up her hand. "Wait. There's more. The vice president was none other than Tessa Lafferty."

Now that was a turn of events that led to all sorts of fascinating possibilities. It even fit quite nicely with Molly's belief that Tessa had been desperate to prove herself in business. The only question now was who, besides Clark Dupree, had known about Tessa's involvement in Danson Properties.

CHAPTER
SEVENTEEN

Liza was all for driving straight to Clark Dupree's office and stabbing him in the heart. It took Molly and Jeannette combined to restrain her.

"Two murders don't make a right," Molly reminded her. "We don't know that he killed Tessa. Why would he, if she was his partner?"

"I don't give a damn whether he killed Tessa. He's trying to rape the Everglades. He sat right there today and swore he was not representing Danson Properties."

"He's probably not," Molly said. "Only a fool would represent himself. Isn't that the way the saying goes?"

"More or less," Liza agreed. "But that's a technicality. He basically lied to us. When the others hear about this, they'll want to lynch him."

Molly could believe that. "Which may explain why he declined to comment today," she said dryly. "Would you admit to this in a hostile crowd?"

Liza sagged back into her chair. "No. Do you think Patrice knew? Could this be the reason she was so furious with him?"

"You mean this on top of the fact that he was screwing Tessa?"

"To a woman of principle like Patrice, this would probably matter more."

"Based on her reaction earlier, I'd say she might have suspected he was involved with Danson, but I don't think she knew even that for certain, much less knew that he actually owned the company."

"What if Tessa hadn't realized exactly what Danson Properties was buying into?" Liza suggested slowly. "What if she found out and confronted him that night? They argued and Tessa ended up in the bay."

Molly had considered the same possibility and dismissed it. "I have a hard time picturing Tessa morally outraged enough to blow a gasket over Clark's development deals, especially when it was her first big shot at proving her worth as a businesswoman. I know she was on record as an environmentalist, but I had the feeling that, like Helen Whorton, she took that position because it was politically correct. Am I wrong?"

"Not entirely," Liza said dully. "Too bad, though. I liked that scenario."

"I have a better one," Molly soothed. "What if she found out, maybe Clark even revealed it to her in some intimate moment, and she tried to blackmail him. Clark's always had the law on his side when he's gone into these fights. He's always sounded very high and mighty, stating that everyone under our system of justice deserves the best representation he or she can get. He's acted as if it weren't something he personally would ever do, right?"

"The same argument given by those who defend drug dealers and rapists," Liza said in disgust.

"But the point is he's never been involved himself. In fact, he's gone to the extreme of forking over huge donations to politically correct environmental causes."

"As if that would make up for his choice of clients," Liza grumbled.

"True, but that's not what I'm getting at," Molly said. "I seriously doubt he'd want it known that he was trying to develop the Everglades at the same time he's sitting on a board that's committed to protecting it. Tessa and Roger needed money. We know that. This deal might have held out the promise of a solution. Then when she realized what she'd gotten herself into, she might have tried blackmailing Clark. He strikes me as sleazy enough to murder her to keep her quiet. Maybe she simply tried to bail out, but he wouldn't let her."

"You know what I think of him," Liza said. "But we don't have any proof. All we have is an interesting theory."

The door to Molly's office opened just then. Michael stepped in and beamed at the two of them. "Just in time, I see."

"Just in time for what?"

"To keep you two from dashing off to prove whatever theory it is you've dreamed up. Care to share it with me?"

With some reluctance, Molly recited everything they'd been able to piece together since the meeting earlier in the afternoon. To her surprise, Michael nodded approvingly.

"Good work. That could fit with another piece of evidence we picked up today. Abrams got a call from the captain of a yacht that was cruising on Biscayne Bay Saturday night. He'd taken a party to Bimini and didn't read about the murder until he got back."

"And?"

"He says he heard an argument about the time of the murder. He couldn't be sure because of the way voices carry on the water, but it seemed to be coming from the grounds of Vizcaya. It was a man and woman, but he couldn't tell any more than that."

"So it might have been Clark and Tessa," Molly said.

"But why didn't anyone else hear them?"

Michael shook his head. "Could be the way the wind was blowing. Could have been the music drowned them out."

"The only thing that puzzles me is how Clark would get a candlestick down to the water without Tessa noticing."

"He didn't," Michael said. "Or, rather, the killer didn't. There wasn't a trace of anything to link that to the murder. The wound didn't match either, according to the medical examiner. It wasn't made by something with sharp edges."

"Then why was it missing?"

"For all we know it was never even there. Maybe it had never left Neville's office."

"Believe me," Liza said. "Neville knew exactly what was in that truck when he brought it to Vizcaya. He's fanatical about details like that."

"Then my guess would be that one of Neville's employees figured it was valuable and tucked it away to be fenced later. When he heard rumors that the police thought it might have been the murder weapon, he slipped it back into Neville's office. At any rate, whatever the killer did use to hit Tessa is probably at the bottom of the bay. It wouldn't have taken much to knock her unconscious. A good-sized rock would have done the trick. The blow didn't kill her."

226

"What then?" Molly asked.

"The medical examiner speculates that she might have come to at some point, but in the dark, tangled in those mangroves and disoriented, she drowned before she could free herself. There was evidence that she'd struggled, but the scratches were more consistent with scrapes she would have sustained underwater than with any she might have gotten in a fight."

"Oh, God," Molly murmured, horrified by the image of such a tortured death. Liza looked equally shaken.

"How could Clark have thrown her in there and walked away, knowing she might still be alive?" Liza said. "What kind of man would do that?"

"One who was desperate," Michael said. "And we don't know it was Clark Dupree. Until we do, you'd be wise not to speculate in public. He's the kind that will sue you for slander, if you're wrong."

"I doubt I'm wrong," Liza said. "But I'll keep my opinion to myself."

The door to the office, already partially open, was flung wide. Expecting Vince or Jeannette, Molly was dismayed to see Hal DeWitt standing there glaring at her. If the judgmental expression on his face was anything to go by, he'd overhead enough of the conversation to guess what it was about.

"You just can't leave it alone, can you?" he said wearily.

Molly cast a look of pure desperation at Liza and Michael, but they were already on their feet. At least Michael looked torn about leaving her alone with her ex-husband. That didn't stop him from going, though. He gave her a supportive thumbs-up sign from the doorway.

When they'd gone, she felt abandoned. She also felt more frightened than she ever had in her life as she met Hal's furious gaze.

"Why are you here?" she asked.

"I thought we should talk again about the custody suit."

Molly's breath caught in her throat. "You've decided something?"

"I thought I had," he admitted, sinking wearily into the chair just vacated by Michael.

He closed his eyes and rubbed his temples, as if he was fighting a pounding headache. The tension in Molly's neck promised a headache of her own as she waited for his verdict, a decision that could dramatically affect her life and Brian's.

When Hal finally looked at her again, he said, "Until I walked in that door just now, I was ready to let it go. I'd convinced myself after our talk the other night that you wouldn't knowingly put Brian in danger and that I was overreacting. Then I walk in here and find you plotting and scheming to catch a killer."

"We were talking, batting around ideas," she retorted, trying to make him see reason. It was never an easy task with Hal, especially when he was in a self-righteous mood. "That's hardly dangerous. One of the people involved in that discussion is a police officer."

"The same police officer who hasn't had sense enough to keep you from snooping around in those other two cases. Am I right?"

"Don't try to blame my involvement on Michael."

"Oh, I'm sure you jumped into the fray all on your own. But he could have told you to take a hike, instead of sitting around discussing the case with you, keeping you all churned up about it. What kind of policeman would do that? I ought to have the guy checked out."

"Leave Michael out of this. He's not involved in our situation. And, I repeat, there is nothing dangerous about comparing notes and exchanging ideas," she said, clinging desperately to her last shred of patience.

"It is if all that talk reaches the ears of the wrong person. I may not be a criminal lawyer, Molly, but I've seen more than my share of murder cases that hinged on the testimony of one key witness. In quite a few of those cases that witness wound up just as dead as the original victim. Why do you think they have witness protection programs?"

He looked her in the eye, his gaze unflinching. "I don't want that to happen to you. I really don't," he said flatly. "I won't allow it to happen to Brian." He got slowly to his feet. "I guess I'll see you in court, after all."

Stunned by the finality in his voice, she tried to prevent him from leaving, but to no avail. He wouldn't even glance back at her on his way out the door.

"Oh, God," she whispered, burying her head in her hands as Michael and Liza edged back into the office.

"What happened?" Liza asked, regarding her sympathetically.

"Molly?" Michael said gently when she didn't respond.

She glanced up, blinking back tears. "He was going to drop the custody suit."

"*Was* going to?" Liza said.

Molly nodded. "He overheard what we were saying and decided I hadn't learned my lesson, after all. He's going to court."

"He won't win," Michael said firmly. He perched on the edge of her desk and cupped her chin in his hand until she was forced to meet his gaze. "No court would take Brian away from you, okay?"

She wanted to believe him, but Hal had a certain amount of power at the courthouse. "I can't be sure of that. You've never heard Hal in court.

He's a brilliant litigator. By the time he's finished, I'll come out sounding like the mother from hell."

"You're forgetting one thing," Michael reminded her, brushing away an errant tear with the pad of his thumb.

"What's that?"

"Brian."

"That's right," Liza said. "Brian doesn't want to live with his father. He also has plenty of details to prove that Hal's interest in his welfare is somewhat belated. How many times has Hal canceled his visits? How many birthday presents came a week late? Or not at all?"

"I'm not sure a judge will compare a missing toy with murder investigations and rule in my favor," Molly said bleakly.

"He will if I have anything to say about it," Michael said, his voice filled with cold, hard determination. "If need be, I can pull in half a dozen cops who are also full-time mothers. Nobody's challenging their ability as parents."

"Maybe because they carry guns," Molly retorted, but she was beginning to feel more encouraged.

"If you think I'm standing by and watching you get a gun, you're crazy," Liza declared. "We have too many on the streets as it is."

Michael grinned. "I don't think we have to

arm Molly to prove to the court she's a capable mother.''

"Thank you, I think," she said dryly.

He regarded her intently. "Are you okay with this now?"

"I'm ready to fight, if that's what you mean."

"Good. Then I want to take off and pay a visit to Clark Dupree."

"Not without me," Molly said.

"Don't you think this would be a good time to go home and spend a little time with your son?" he said. "I promise I'll come by right after the meeting and fill you in on every detail."

Reason won out over curiosity. If Hal decided to spring his decision on Brian tonight, her son would need her. Michael, on the other hand, hardly needed her assistance in questioning a suspect. He'd had more practice.

"You'll come by?"

"I said I would."

She nodded. "Then hurry. My curiosity will be killing me. Liza?"

Her friend looked torn. "I'd really like to hear what Clark has to say, if Michael doesn't mind."

"Actually your presence might make it more likely that he'll slip up. I have no objection to your coming along."

"Molly?" Liza said.

"Oh, go ahead. There's no reason for two of us to be biting our nails."

She followed them to the parking lot, then watched them start toward Michael's car. They were almost there when he hesitated, then turned and walked back toward her.

Hands stuffed in his pockets, he stood gazing down at her intently. "Give Brian an extra hug for me, okay?"

Tears sprang to Molly's eyes again. "Yeah. I'll do that," she promised.

He nodded in satisfaction, then went back to join Liza. Molly stood staring after them until his car was out of sight, heading north toward Clark Dupree's Brickell Avenue office.

CHAPTER
EIGHTEEN

Unfortunately, Clark Dupree wasn't in his Brickell Avenue office. He was waiting in the lobby of Molly's Key Biscayne condominium. He looked as if he'd settled in for a long wait.

Nestor, the Nicaraguan head of security for Ocean Manor, had his eyes on the well-dressed interloper who'd made himself at home on the lobby sofa and was sifting through the papers in his fancy briefcase. Nestor's worried expression deepened as he latched on to Molly's arm and dragged her back outside.

"He ask for you, then for Ms. Hastings. When I tell him you are not here, he say he wait. There is something about the man." He shook his head. "I do not like him. Should I call Señor Michael?"

Molly wasn't wild about the idea that Nestor

thought she needed rescuing or that he regarded Michael as her savior in all slightly tricky situations. At the same time, it seemed foolish not to let Michael know that his chief suspect was sitting in her lobby.

"Call him," she told Nestor, giving him Michael's car phone number. She tried very hard not to make it sound urgent. She didn't want Michael roaring in here with sirens blasting. "Tell him I'll talk with Mr. Dupree right here in the lobby until he arrives."

She plastered a smile on her face, crossed the lobby, and took a chair next to Clark. "I understand you're looking for me or Liza."

Clark rose slowly. At his six-foot-two-inch height, he was an imposing figure. Normally, in social situations anyway, he sought to temper that impression with soft-spoken charm. Today, however, his smile seemed forced.

"Yes," he said, sitting again once she was settled. "I understand you were looking for me earlier in the week. I had business on the Key and thought I'd drop by to see what you wanted. When the guard said you were out, I asked for Liza. After the meeting this afternoon, I'm sure she has questions for me as well."

"About Danson, you mean?"

He nodded. "You both know by now, I assume."

"We checked out the incorporation records, yes."

"Then you know that I am president of Danson Properties and that Tessa was the vice president." He glanced around the lobby with distaste, an expression that would have appalled those who fought so valiantly for this particular flowery decor. "Could we possibly discuss this upstairs? I really don't like discussing business in the middle of a public lobby like this."

Since the lobby was virtually deserted, Molly thought his request a bit unnecessary. Unless, of course, he was getting very nervous about how much she knew and wanted to clobber her over the head in private. Just in case, she didn't think she'd allow him that opportunity.

She managed a smile. "Actually, it's a lot quieter here than it would be upstairs. My son and his friends are in my apartment. You don't join a group of third-graders if you want peace and quiet."

He took the rejection fairly well. "Perhaps we could go for coffee, then?"

Molly refused to acknowledge the twinge of worry that was beginning to nag at her. Clark might have killed Tessa, but she didn't know that for sure. Besides, what could possibly happen with Nestor not twenty yards away? She simply had to keep him here and talking until Michael arrived.

Maybe she could even wrangle a confession out of him.

"Mr. Dupree, I really don't see what we have to discuss," she said, hoping to persuade him that she knew absolutely nothing incriminating about him and wasn't the least bit involved in the investigation. "Your business dealings are no affair of mine, and while I happen to agree with the stance the coalition has taken in the past with regard to the Everglades, I have no official capacity with that organization."

"I think we do share one common interest, however."

"Which is?"

"Discovering who murdered Tessa."

Molly blinked at the smooth delivery. Wouldn't the killer have had a hard time making that remark seem convincing? Was it possible that she and Liza were wrong about Clark, after all?

"Did you and Tessa argue the night of the gala?" she asked point-blank, hoping to startle him into a slip.

Again, he smiled faintly. "You see, I was right. You are interested."

"Of course I'm interested," she said a trifle impatiently, seeing no need to continue her charade. It hadn't worked anyway. "I discovered Tessa's body. It's not something I'm likely to get over in a hurry. It would help to know who was responsible for her death."

"Then please, let's go for coffee. I'll tell you everything I know about what happened that night. You pick the place. We can even take separate cars," he added, giving her a wry look that told her he knew exactly what she was thinking. While he might consider her fears foolish, he obviously intended to humor her, to make it difficult for her to decline the invitation.

In fact, how could she possibly refuse when it seemed unlikely that she would actually have to be alone with him? She could drive to one of the hotels, the Sheraton or the Sonesta, valet park, and meet him in a coffee shop or the bar. He could hardly run her off the road and shoot her on busy Crandon Boulevard without risking immediate capture.

"We'll go to the Sheraton," she said finally. With its French doors facing the ocean, the restaurant was so well lit it was impossible to imagine a less ominous setting. "I'll meet you there."

"Thank you."

Just to make sure he knew she was leaving a trail, she pointedly told Nestor that she would be at the nearby hotel if Brian or anyone else came looking for her.

Nestor gave her a reluctant nod, indicating that he understood the full implications of her request, even if he wasn't wild about her departure. "I will tell them." He glanced at Clark Dupree. "You wish me to tell Ms. Hastings you are there, if she returns?"

"Why not?" Clark said agreeably. "The more the merrier."

As Molly drove the few blocks to the ocean-front hotel, she tried to figure out exactly what Clark Dupree was up to. Was he merely trying to invoke some sympathy for his own position as the distraught, bereaved lover? Was he genuinely after Tessa's killer? Or was he simply trying to determine exactly how much Molly knew so he could decide if she posed a danger to him?

Her own reaction to the man was unexpected. She despised his values and she was wary, but she wasn't afraid. Hopefully her gut instincts were fully operational after the round she'd gone with Hal earlier. Hopefully Michael and Liza would show up before she had to find out.

Inside the hotel, Clark made no objections to entering the airy restaurant, which was quieter than Molly might have liked. They chose a table by the doors, which were open to admit the sea breeze. Molly ordered coffee and Clark ordered a martini straight up. Apparently he needed false fortitude for whatever he had to tell her.

"I asked you earlier if you and Tessa had argued the night she was killed," Molly said when he showed no inclination to get started.

"Tessa and I always argued. It was part of her fascination for me that she never backed down from her strong opinions. I value that strength of character in anyone.''

"Did her opinions have some validity?"

"Sometimes. In other instances, her pigheadedness almost drove me crazy.''

"Was she right about Danson Properties, in your opinion? Or was she merely being pig-headed, as you put it?"

He stared off toward the window that faced the Atlantic, a faraway look in his eyes. He appeared almost as if he might be overcome with emotion, but when he blinked and gazed back at Molly there was every indication that his usual reserve was firmly in place.

"How much do you know about Tessa and Roger's financial difficulties?"

"Very little, except that they were in some trouble.''

"Tessa had been investing in the stock market, junk bonds as it turns out. She was always so sure of herself, so supremely confident of her business acumen. She was ripe for some unscrupulous broker to rob her blind.''

"Did Roger know?"

"He learned far too late to prevent disaster from striking. She'd gone through her inheritance and was well into debt for an amount equal to most of his cash reserves when he caught on and called a halt to things. He threatened to have the broker brought up on charges, but it was an idle threat. In such situations, fraud is difficult to prove. Naturally, Tessa was humiliated by the whole affair.''

"And I'm sure Roger was furious.''

"Perhaps so, but he didn't let her know how he felt. He simply tried to clean up the mess. That's the kind of man Roger is. Honorable to a fault.''

"Honorable? I heard he took out an insurance policy on Tessa.''

Clark shook his head ruefully. "So you know about that? Actually, the policy was Tessa's idea, a way to make amends.''

"Eventually,'' Molly pointed out.

"Yes, eventually.''

"What does all this have to do with Danson Properties?''

"When the federal authorities began making changes in the laws governing the wetlands, I heard talk starting up about the area again and I saw an opportunity. I began buying up land. I knew about Tessa's difficulties and I offered to cut her in on the deal.''

"Did she know where this property was?''

His shoulders slumped dejectedly. "Not until the night of the gala.''

"How did she find out?''

"She didn't. Roger did. He mentioned it to her in passing, outraged by the notion that a company was poised to destroy a part of the Everglades again. When he mentioned the name of the company, I gather she almost fainted. By the time I saw her Saturday night, she was livid.''

Molly could imagine the confrontation. Tessa, thinking that she had taken a step that might make up for her earlier business disasters, had discovered that instead she had made an even more grievous mistake. Realizing that her lover had intentionally deceived her about the nature of their development plans must have cut her to the quick.

''What did she want you to do?''

''She wanted me to sell the property to the coalition and walk away.''

''You refused,'' Molly guessed.

''Actually I might have considered it. I would have done anything for Tessa,'' he said with unmistakable sincerity. ''I only involved her in this deal to try to save her pride. I didn't think it through. I never realized how deeply she felt about the coalition. Not many people did. They thought she was shallow. The worst thing was, she knew that. I think that's what made her so angry about this deal, because she knew her detractors would see it as proof that she had caved in when it was expedient for her to do so.''

Molly was trying to revise her opinions of Tessa and Clark, to put them in perspective in light of what she'd learned and what had happened next. If she bought his story, then it seemed terribly unlikely that he would have killed her. "What happened that night?" she asked. "After you argued, Clark, what happened next?"

His shoulders slumped in defeat. "I don't know," he said wearily. "I wish to God I did, but I don't. When I walked away from Tessa, she was angry, but she was very much alive. I swear it."

Molly gazed directly at him, until he lifted his eyes to meet hers. She saw agony in the brown depths, agony and sorrow, but not guilt. Her gut instincts were certain of that much at least.

"Tell me again everything that you and Tessa said that night," she suggested as an idea began to take shape in her mind. It was the only thing that made a sad kind of sense. Slowly, Clark recounted the argument from beginning to end, the revelations about the development deal, Tessa's furious accusations, his own desperate attempts to placate her.

"I told her that I loved her, that I would never have intentionally hurt her."

"What did she say then?"

"She said it was too bad, that she had loved me, too, but it was over between us. She said she would never be able to trust me again."

"So it would have been clear to anyone overhearing the fight that you and Tessa had been lovers?"

"I suppose so, yes," he said thoughtfully. Then as awareness of her point dawned, he whispered, "Roger. You think Roger heard it all and killed her for betraying him."

"He worshiped her. You were his best friend. It makes sense that he would be furious, that it might be the one thing he could never forgive."

"But there were others before me," he protested, albeit weakly.

Molly recalled the expression on Roger's face that day at the house as he regarded Clark with total contempt, the look of a man deeply betrayed on all levels. "None of them were Roger's best friend," she reminded him.

An odd transformation came over Clark then. It was as if all of his own pain gave way to a cold, hard anger. Molly had never seen anything like it before in her life and it sent a shiver down her back.

He raised his hand for the check, handed the waiter the money, and nodded at Molly, his expression already a little distant. "Thank you for joining me," he said politely, but with absolutely no feeling in his tone. Even his gaze had gone blank.

As he walked away from the table, Molly knew where he was going.

She also knew what he was planning to do.

CHAPTER
NINETEEN

Where the hell was Michael? Molly thought as she raced across the hotel lobby and out the door. She wondered if it was possible to arrest someone *before* they committed a crime.

Clark hadn't bothered with valet parking and was already heading for his car, his long-legged strides giving him a distinct advantage over her. Unless he chose to let her, she would never catch up with him on foot. Her only hope would be to follow in her car, using her cellular phone to try to reach Michael and Roger to warn them of Clark Dupree's apparent intentions.

Clark's black Lexus sped from the parking lot, hitting the speed bump at full throttle. It was a wonder he didn't knock himself unconscious on the roof, Molly thought watching him as she waited impatiently for her own car.

Fortunately there was only one route off of the Key. If he was, in fact, headed to the Gables, she would have ample opportunity to catch up with him. As she turned onto Crandon Boulevard, heading northwest toward the mainland, she was already punching in Michael's number.

"Come on," she muttered when he didn't pick up immediately. "Dammit, Michael, pick up."

While she listened to the distant ring, she fumbled with her address book, trying to locate the Laffertys' number. As soon as she found it, she disconnected the failed call to Michael and tried to reach Roger. Josie answered. She sounded thoroughly worn out.

"Mr. Roger isn't here, miss. He's been coming home late most nights, if he comes home at all."

"Do you know where he might be?"

"His office, maybe. Or the country club. Sometimes he goes by there."

"Thanks, Josie." She hesitated, trying to find a way to warn the housekeeper about Clark without alarming her. "Josie, if Mr. Dupree comes by, don't tell him where you think Mr. Lafferty might be, okay?"

"Why not?" she asked, sounding puzzled. "They been good friends a long time now. Mr.

Roger needs his friends around him at a time like this.''

"Mr. Dupree is very upset about something right now. I just don't think it would be the best time for them to talk. If Mr. Lafferty comes home, tell him the same thing. Please, Josie.''

Fortunately the housekeeper had spent a lifetime taking orders from a woman even more of a mystery than Molly. She considered it her duty to follow instructions to the letter, no matter what she thought of them. "Yes, ma'am. I'll tell him.''

Molly tried Michael again. Still he didn't answer. Where could he be? Whenever he wasn't in the car, he carried that pocket-sized cellular phone with him. That wonder of the technological age was on its tenth or twelfth ring, when a tentative, vaguely familiar voice answered. *"Bueno!"*

"Nestor?'' Molly said slowly, fighting astonishment and confusion.

"Sí. This is Nestor.''

"Nestor, it's Mrs. DeWitt. Where is Michael?''

"Here,'' he said, sounding distressed. "He and Mr. DeWitt, they are fighting.''

"Michael and Hal are fighting?'' she said, torn between incredulity and dismay. "You mean brawling? A fistfight?'' It was beyond her comprehension.

"No fists. They shout. Very loud. They do not hear the phone. I pick it up.''

"Would you tell those two macho jerks to shut up? I need Michael now!"

The urgency in her voice got through to him. "*Sí. Sí.* I tell them."

He put the phone down. Molly could hear his voice climb, issuing commands in Spanish. Then she heard Michael's rapid-fire response, counterpointed by Hal's querulous demands to know what was going on. His stubborn refusal to learn Spanish had put him at a distinct disadvantage, and he was clearly making his dissatisfaction known.

"Molly?" Michael said finally. "Where are you? What's going on?"

She summarized her suspicions as succinctly as possible.

"I'll call Abrams," he promised. "I'm on my way. Molly, don't you dare get in the middle of this. Turn around and come home."

"Not on your life. I will not let Clark Dupree waltz in and kill Roger while you rally the troops."

"How do you intend to stop them? By talking them both to death?"

"Very funny. I've already warned Josie not to tell Clark where Roger might be. In case he does come home before Clark gets there, I've told her to warn him."

"Good going, but that's enough. The police will take it from here."

"The police will take it from here if you stop

arguing with me and get moving. Otherwise, I figure I'm on my own. I'm almost to the Lafferty house now and Clark was ahead of me."

He sighed deeply, clearly sensing that her formidible resolve had kicked in. "Promise me you'll stay out of the line of fire, *amiga*. If you go getting yourself killed, we'll never know how all this flirting will end up."

Molly knew exactly where all the flirting was headed. She just didn't know the timetable. She intended to be around for the finale, though. "I'll be careful," she promised.

She heard Hal's shouted demand to know what was going on just as the phone clicked off. Her car phone rang within minutes.

"Molly," Hal said, sounding breathless.

Either the fight had taken its toll or he'd raced to his own car phone. He was definitely on the road. She could hear the sounds of traffic, the impatient blaring of his horn.

"Where are you and what is happening?" he demanded.

She gave him an abbreviated version of the same story.

"Clark Dupree is going after Roger? I don't believe it."

"Why? Because attorneys never turn into criminals?" she inquired sarcastically. "I could name a few who engage in criminal behavior all the time."

"Not murder," he said piously. "And we're talking about Clark Dupree here. He's a model citizen."

"A model citizen who was intending to rape the Everglades. A model citizen who was having an affair with his best friend's wife. I actually think he was in love with Tessa. He flipped out when he realized Roger might have killed her."

"Then let the police and the shrinks have at him. Go home to your son."

"That's exactly what I intend to do . . . if they get there in time. Hal, I can't talk to you and drive at the same time. We'll talk later."

"Molly! Molly, don't you dare hang up on me!"

She ignored the order.

It was less easy to ignore the panic and desperation she'd heard in his tone. Maybe she was going to have to admit at last that Hal DeWitt still loved her enough to be terrified for her. Her own feelings toward him were less clear and now was certainly not the time to analyze them. The only thing that did occur to her was that while Michael clearly worried about her, he usually trusted her to use her head in a crisis. That pretty much summed up the difference in the two relationships. Hal still thought she had no more judgment than a head of lettuce.

As she rounded the corner onto Roger's street in the Gables, she saw Clark's car turning into the drive, saw the guard wave him in, and realized that she hadn't thought to tell Josie to warn the guard. She took the turn into the drive-way on two wheels and squealed to a stop right behind the fancy black car. There was no sign of Roger's car. Hopefully he still hadn't come home.

"Clark!" Molly shouted as she climbed out of the car.

The guard cast a startled look in her direction. It was a new guard, one she'd never seen before, though Clark obviously had.

"Is something wrong, miss?" he said, coming toward her.

"He's after Mr. Lafferty. I think he's planning to kill him," she said. "The police are on their way."

Just then Clark spun around as if he'd heard the words she'd spoken in a deliberate under-tone. He looked distraught. "Why did you come?"

"I had to try to talk you out of doing some-thing you'd regret for the rest of your life," Molly said, staying behind the door of her car. It offered scant protection, but it was better than nothing, especially since it was clear that he'd traded his briefcase for a gun. He held it steadily in front of him, aimed in her direction. The guard was try-ing to inch around behind him, so Molly forced herself to keep talking.

"I know how terrible it must be for you,

knowing that Roger killed the woman you loved, but the police will catch him and the courts will see that he's punished.''

An odd expression passed over his face, an expression that suddenly had Molly doubting everything she'd surmised over the past couple of hours. Stunned by how badly she'd misread things, she simply stared as he began moving toward her.

''I added it up all wrong, didn't I?'' she said with dawning understanding. She was conscious of every slow, careful movement behind Clark as the guard got into position. ''You're not here to kill Roger because he murdered Tessa, are you? You want him dead because he saw what really happened that night.''

''Very good, Mrs. DeWitt,'' he said as if she'd mastered a very difficult lesson. ''I thought I had you fooled. It was only as we talked that I realized you were right, that Roger must have seen everything, including the fact that Tessa and I struggled, that I grabbed up a rock, knocked her unconscious, and dumped her into the bay.''

''But he told no one what he'd seen that night,'' Molly reminded him, trying not to glance in the direction of the guard who was just about ready to pounce and strip Clark of his gun. ''He remained your friend, despite everything you'd done to him.''

Clark's laughter sent chills down Molly's spine.

"Friend? If he was there that night, he knew what it would do to me to wait for him to reveal everything. He wasn't being noble, Mrs. DeWitt. He was torturing me, making me wait, letting the guilt work on me."

"That's right," said a voice from behind Molly. As Clark's attention shifted, she recognized the cool, controlled voice of Roger Lafferty, sounding more certain than he had at any time since the devastating events of Saturday night. "And now you're going to pay."

Molly whirled around just in time to see the flash of gunfire, smell the acrid scent of gunpowder. Expecting a volley of shots to be fired, she hit the ground, but there was only the one blast and then quiet fell behind the protective gates that had failed in their job to keep this household safe after all. She dared to peek and saw that Roger Lafferty had laid the gun on the trunk of her car and was slumped over. She glanced around the car door and saw Clark Dupree on the ground, the security guard hovering over him. Clark was writhing, clutching his leg, so the wound probably wasn't fatal.

Molly reached into the car, grabbed her cellular phone and called 911, just as Michael's car turned into the driveway. Hal's was right on its tail, despite the fact that he must have been speeding the whole way to keep up. She was surprised there wasn't an entire fleet of Coral Gables patrol cars in their wake.

Michael took in the scene at a glance, retrieved Roger's gun, then pulled her into his arms the instant he was assured that the key players were disarmed. "I see you have everything under control," he said dryly.

"Not quite," she admitted, understanding now why she could never walk away from whatever the future might have in store for the two of them. Michael was strong, but more than that, he gave her strength. "I had it wrong. Clark was guilty, after all. Roger saw him murder Tessa. That's why Clark came over here to kill him."

She glanced at Roger and saw a broken man, a man who had lost everything that ever mattered to him in a period of a few days. "The only thing I don't understand is why you didn't try to save her," she said to him.

Roger regarded her wearily. "Don't you see? I couldn't. I felt so betrayed, so angry. In the end, you see, I am every bit as guilty as Clark."

Hal had gone to Clark's side and Molly heard him ask if he wanted a lawyer. "I'll call someone for you," he offered.

Clark shook his head. "No. It's over for me. There's no point in doing anything other than pleading guilty. I can certainly do that on my own."

Molly figured it would be a new experience since he usually plea-bargained his clients out of paying for their crimes.

Hal turned finally and walked slowly in her direction. Michael looked from Molly to her ex-husband and back again. He gave her shoulders a squeeze and went to explain what had happened to Detective Abrams, who'd just arrived on the scene. Molly was left alone to face her ex-husband.

Pale and clearly shaken, Hal shoved his hands into his pockets. His gaze surveyed her hungrily as if he needed desperately to assure himself that she was really all right. "You're okay?" he asked, as if he feared his eyes might deceive him.

"Fine."

"You deliberately led Clark away from Brian, didn't you?"

"You mean by taking him to the Sheraton?"

He nodded.

"That was part of it. If he had had anything desperate in mind, I didn't want it to happen around Brian. But to be honest, it was more than that. I also could see he wouldn't talk where we were and I had to know what had really happened to Tessa."

"You couldn't wait to read it in the paper like the rest of us?"

She shook her head. "From the minute I found her body, this wasn't some news story to me. It was personal. If it could happen to Tessa in the middle of a fund-raiser, then it could happen to anyone." She drew in a breath and admitted what was at the heart of everything. "It could happen to me."

His gaze narrowed. "Don't you see? That's what terrifies me."

"I know you worry. I can't blame you for that. But when I look for the answers behind something like Tessa's murder or Greg Kinsey's or Allan Winecroft's, I feel in control again. I feel like I'm getting an edge up on anyone who might ever try to hurt me or Brian."

Hal nodded slowly. "I guess I can understand that. It's a scary world out there these days. We all need to do whatever we can to be in control of our lives. I suppose that's all I was doing by filing this custody suit."

Molly stepped closer and touched his cheek, wishing that it had never come to this sad state of affairs between them, but knowing that there was no way to go back. "Maybe there's a solution for us short of taking this to court. Now that we both understand where we're coming from, next time, if there is a next time, I will bring Brian to stay with you. That way we'll both know that he's out of harm's way."

"You've never been willing to do that before," he said, sounding surprised by the gesture.

"Because I was always afraid you wouldn't

bring him back," she admitted. "Do we have a deal, Hal?"

He cupped her face in his hands and for an instant she was certain he intended to kiss her. Instead he merely leveled an intense gaze directly into her eyes, then smiled faintly.

"We have a deal." He brushed a kiss on her forehead. "I suppose it doesn't hurt that you have a cop standing by, if things get really out of hand." He shot a grudging glance of respect at Michael, who was hovering a discreet distance away. "Take care of her, O'Hara."

Michael slid his arm around her waist. "She doesn't need me to do that, DeWitt. She can take care of herself." He grinned down at her. "Right, amiga?"

Darn right.

Nature always has the last word.

John Stewart Collis

Watch for the next Molly DeWitt
romantic mystery, *HOT SCHEMES,*
coming next winter from Dell.

CHAPTER
ONE

The deafening music pulsed to a Latin beat at Sundays on the Bay. Molly DeWitt had long since given up any attempts to carry on a conversation with Michael O'Hara, whose attention seemed to be focused more on the horizon than on her anyway. His beer sat untouched, warming in the sun. As near as she could tell, with his eyes shaded by his favorite reflective sunglasses, he hadn't even noticed the five scantily clad women at the next table. That's how she knew he was far more worried than he was letting on.

"Still no sign of your uncle's boat?" she shouted over the music.

He glanced at her briefly, shook his head, then turned his attention back to the water. His expression was more somber than she'd ever seen it, even in the midst of some particularly grue-some homicide investigations.

Molly understood his concern. It was now af-ter 4:00 P.M. Tío Miguel should have been back by two o'clock, three at the latest, from his regular Sunday fishing trip. By then he would usually have enough snapper or grouper for the family's dinner, plus extra to share with friends up and down the block in their Little Havana neighbor-hood.

The rest of the week Tío Miguel worked nights delivering the morning newspaper door to door, then took out fishing charters, usually wealthy Latin Americans and their Miami busi-ness associates.

A small, olive-complexioned man with dark-as-midnight eyes, Miguel García had an unmistak-able wiry strength even though he was about to turn sixty-five. Molly had met him several months earlier at dinner at Tío Pedro's, yet another of Michael's uncles. She had been instantly charmed by his softspoken blending of English and Span-ish and the pride in his voice as he talked of Mi-chael's accomplishments in Miami.

Tío Miguel and Tío Pedro and their wives—both sisters of Michael's mother—had preceded Michael to Miami when Fidel Castro overthrew Batista in Cuba. They had left behind homes, family, and once-thriving careers in the hope of regaining freedom. It was to them, via one of the famed Pedro Pan airlifts, that Michael's mother had sent him, alone at the age of five.

Though Molly had known other exiles, none had touched her quite the way Tío Miguel had. When he talked of his native land, there had been such sadness in his eyes and something more, an anger perhaps, that his homeland was out of reach to him now. Unlike his brother, who owned a flourishing Cuban restaurant, Tío Miguel had never fully adapted to his new land.

Like so many other Cuban exiles who had come to Miami in the sixties, Tío Miguel had struggled with English. Fortunately, he lived in a community where shopkeepers spoke Spanish, where parish priests and government officials spoke his language. He had settled for taking menial jobs to support his family, always with the fragile hope that he would return home to a free Cuba someday. As time passed, hope had faded.

Molly glanced at Michael and saw that his attention was still avidly focused on Biscayne Bay and the Atlantic beyond.

"You're worried, aren't you?" she said.

"He's never been this late before."

"Does he have a radio on the boat?"

Michael nodded.

"Then he can call the Coast Guard if he's in trouble. I'm sure he's okay. He probably found a hot spot where the fish were really biting and didn't want to come in yet."

"Maybe," he said tersely. He stood up. "I'm going inside to make a call. Keep an eye out for him, will you?"

"Of course."

Though Tío Miguel had invited Michael, Molly, and her son, Brian, to come fishing with him some Sunday, they had never taken him up on it. Brian had brought it up once or twice, but Molly had discouraged him from pressing Michael about it. Now as she watched the endless rows of sailboats, yachts, and fishing boats dotting the water, she realized she had no idea what his boat was named, much less what it looked like. Except for those with billowing sails, they all looked pretty much alike to her, especially from this distance.

When Michael finally returned, if anything he looked more tense.

"What did you find out?"

"Nothing. Tía Pilar said she was expecting him home by now. There was something else in her voice, though, that convinced me I am right to be worried. I called the Coast Guard. They haven't had any distress calls, but they're going out to take a look." He didn't have to say that he'd called in a favor to accomplish that. He drummed his fingers nervously on the table and took another sip of beer. "Damn, I can't stand this. Come on."

"Where?"

"I'll run you home, then rent a boat. I'm going out myself. I've been out with him enough. I probably know better than the Coast Guard does where to start looking." He threw some money on the table, then slipped between the tightly packed tables along the edge of the marina.

They were nearly to the car, when Molly touched his arm. "Michael, I want to go with you," she said, unable to ignore his anxiety. She'd learned long ago that Michael was incapable of asking for help, but that didn't mean he couldn't use a little support from a friend once in a while. Predictably, though, he was already shaking his stubborn Cuban-Irish head.

"No. If there's trouble, I don't want you involved."

"What sort of trouble?" she said.

He just shook his head again, his expression more tight-lipped and obstinate than usual. "You're going home."

Molly made up in determination what she lacked in stature. She planted herself in front of him. "Dammit, Michael O'Hara, don't you pull any of this Latin machismo stuff with me. Two pairs of eyes will be better than one out there. If your uncle is hurt, I might be able to help. You won't be able to manage him and the boat at the same time."

Apparently he decided that arguing would simply waste more precious time. That was the only explanation she could think of for his quick, grudging nod. He changed directions.

Halfway down the marina, a middle-aged fisherman was just unloading his catch. He greeted Michael with a nod. *"Hola."*

Michael began talking to him in Spanish. The only thing Molly understand for certain was Tío Miguel's name, but the man's head bobbed in agreement.

"He'll take us out," Michael told her, already following the man onto the boat. He held out his hand to help Molly aboard. "He and my uncle are friends. He saw him just this morning. He went out as usual about dawn."

"Does Tío Miguel usually fish in the same place?" Molly asked.

"More or less. We might have to do some cruising around though. I assume you don't get seasick. The water looks a little choppy today."

"Let's just say it's probably best if we don't put the idea into my head," she said just as the powerful engine started throbbing beneath them. Her stomach lurched, then settled a bit as they eased out of the dock and into open water. Fresh air replaced gas fumes as they chugged out of the harbor. She tried to ignore the thick, dark clouds gathering in the west and the threat they represented.

"You okay?" Michael asked. "You looked a little green there for a minute."

"I'm fine now."

"I want to get up front to help Raul watch for the boat. You'll be okay back here?"

Molly nodded. "What the name of the boat? I'll watch from here."

"The *Niña Pilar*."

She reached out then and touched his hand. "We'll find him, Michael."

"I hope so," he said and turned abruptly, but not before she'd noted the tense set of his jaw and the deepening worry in his eyes in that instant before he'd slipped his sunglasses back into place.

Not only was he Tío Miguel's namesake, but the two shared a special bond because of Michael's young age when his mother had sent him to America to live with his aunt and uncle. That, combined with the fact that Michael had never known his own Irish-American father, had cemented their relationship. The closeness was not something Michael ever spoke of, but she had learned over the last months to read the emotions in his eyes, even when his words revealed nothing. If something had happened to Tío Miguel, Michael would be devastated, as would the rest of the close-knit family.

Under the glare of the midafternoon sun, a fine mist of salty water dried on Molly's skin almost as soon as it landed. As the boat chugged into deeper seas, the water turned from a glistening silver to a murky green, then purple, darkened from above by the bank of nearly black clouds rolling in, dumping sheets of rain in the distance and hiding the land from sight.

Whether it was due to the afternoon storm itself or Michael's anxiety, Molly grew increasingly uneasy as the boat rocked over the choppy waves. All the other boats were making for land, while they continued to head out to sea.

No longer able to stand being left alone, she made her way forward on the slippery deck, clinging to the metal railing as she climbed up to join Michael and Raul. While the middle-aged Cuban man steered against the powerful northerly currents, a huge cigar clamped between his teeth, Michael kept a pair of borrowed binoculars trained on the horizon.

Molly clung to a railing as the wind ripped at her clothes and tangled her hair. "Any sign of him?"

"Nothing. Raul's heading south."

Molly's uneasiness mounted. "South? Toward Cuba?"

Michael nodded.

Suddenly dozens of stories about ill-fated missions against Castro by fanatical exiles flashed through her mind. "Michael?"

He slowly lowered the binoculars and turned toward her, his expression grim.

"You don't believe he went fishing today, do you?"

"I hope to God I'm wrong, but no."

"But surely he wouldn't . . ."

"He would," Michael said tersely. "The god-damned fool would. He's been involved with some underground group for years. I looked into them once for Tía Pilar. I decided they were harmless enough. I thought that eventually he'd see that there are better ways to end Castro's dictatorship, especially with the fall of communism in the rest of the world."

"But why now, after all this time?" Molly said, unable to imagine the sheer folly of what Michael was suggesting. "You must be wrong. I'm sure he just got caught in a squall or something. He wouldn't try to invade Cuba on his own, for heaven's sake."

"You don't understand what it's been like for him. You can't. Cuba—the Cuba he remembers anyway—is in his soul."

The sadness, Molly thought. That explained the sorrow that perpetually shadowed Tío Miguel's eyes. And Michael was right. It was something she had no way of fully understanding.

"Would he have gone alone, though?" she asked. "Wouldn't there have been others?"

"More than likely, though Raul says he has heard nothing of such plans. Such men operate in secret, but there is almost always gossip."

As the boat churned through the choppy waters, they emerged beneath bluer skies. The wind settled into little more than a breeze that barely stirred the humid tropical air. But even with the improved weather, the tension didn't lessen.

The one question Molly didn't dare to ask was whether Raul would risk carrying them all the way into Cuban waters. Nor was she sure she wanted to know whether Michael would allow him to do any less. Fortunately, with nothing but open water in all directions, Molly had no real sense of how close she might be to having both questions answered.

For all she knew there was little purpose to the zigzagging course they seemed to be on as the sun slipped below the horizon in a blaze of orange.

"There!" Michael said, gesturing to Raul as he kept his binoculars pinned on some tiny speck in the dimming light.

To Molly the boat in the distance was indistinguishable from dozens of others they had seen since leaving the marina. Only as they drew closer did she realize the boat's engine was still, that its movement was propelled by no more than the drifting currents.

"Tío! Tío Miguel!"

Michael's shouts carried across the water as they pulled alongside the boat. *Niña Pilar* had been painted on the boat's bow in neat bright blue letters.

"Can you get any closer?" he asked Raul.

"*Sí,*" he said, maneuvering until the boats were touching.

Michael threw a rope across, then looped it through the railing of his uncle's boat until the two were pontooned together. Only then did he leap from Raul's boat to the deck of his uncle's.

Molly's breath caught in her throat as he made his way carefully from bow to stern. She nearly panicked when he disappeared inside the cabin and failed to return. She had one hand on the railing and was preparing to leap herself, when he reappeared.

"Michael?" she said softly, her heart hammering as she tried to read the expression on his face.

He swallowed hard before he finally lifted his gaze to meet hers.

"He's gone," he said bleakly. "The inflatable raft is missing, too."

"You're sure he's gone back to Cuba, though? Maybe the boat ran out of gas and he took the dinghy to get help," she said, searching desperately for another explanation.

Raul greeted Michael's announcement with a barrage of Spanish. He hurriedly sketched a cross over his chest, his gaze flashing toward heaven. Though she could understand only about one word in ten, something in the fisherman's voice told Molly he disagreed with Michael's interpretation.

Michael questioned him in impatient, rapid-fire Spanish.

"What?" Molly said. "Michael, what is he saying?"

"Muy loco," Michael said derisively to the other man. *"No es posible."*

"Sí," Raul said just as adamantly.

"What, dammit?" Molly said, shouting over the pair of them.

Michael finally looked at her. "Raul seems to think it is not possible that my uncle went back to Cuba."

"Then what does he think happened?"

"He thinks he was murdered," he said in a clipped tone.

"Murdered?"

"You see why I say he is crazy. Who would want to murder an old man who has never done anything to hurt anyone in his life?"

"Can you dismiss what he is saying so easily?" Molly asked, though she didn't want to believe Raul's theory any more than Michael did. "You're a homicide detective, Michael. You of all people know how important it is to look beyond the obvious."

He glared at her. "Maybe just this once I don't want to," he snapped. "Maybe just this

once I don't want to know anything about someone who might be sick enough to hurt an old
man."

"But I know you, Michael. You won't rest until you know the truth. Not about something as
important as this."

A sigh shuddered through him. He slid his
sunglasses back into place though it was long past
any need for them. Without another word, he se-
cured Tío Miguel's boat to be towed back to
Miami, then gestured to Raul.

The fishing boat turned to the north and began chugging through the choppy Atlantic. Molly
could no longer read Michael's expression in the
darkness closing in around them, but he was facing south—toward his homeland. Toward Cuba.

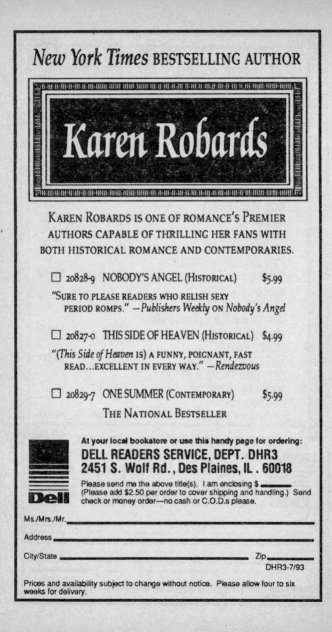